CONSTELIS VOSS VOL. 3:
REFORMAT

CONSTELIS VOSS VOL. 3: REFORMAT

K. LEIGH

k. LEIGH

Editing by Madalyn Rupprecht
Book design by Md. Imran Ahmed
Editing and formatting facilitated by Dr. Rissy's Writing and Marketing
Cover Art by Kira Leigh Maintanis

ISBN: 978-1-7368053-2-9 (paperback)
ASIN: B09BLGB26D (ebook)

https://constelisvoss.ml

k. LEIGH

CONTENTS

"Imagine that you are creating a fabric of human destiny with the object of making men happy in the end, giving them peace and rest at last. Imagine that you are doing this but that it is essential and inevitable to torture to death only one tiny creature...in order to found that edifice on its unavenged tears. Would you consent to be the architect on those conditions? Tell me. Tell the truth."

— Fyodor Dostoevsky, "The Brothers Karamazov".
The Russian Messenger, 1880

You can hate me. I'm fine with you hating me. They can hate me—I deserve it. But I can't have her hating me.

And she will hate me.

Maybe, she'll forgive me, or rather, the me that's out *there*. Considering that he had no fucking choice in the matter, she may yet be sympathetic.

However, as he's a hopeless version of me, he would've done the same as I have. He would've made a decision—one he's made before—in his attempts at 'something awesome.'

A decision to escalate to rectify, try to save his own ass, dole out judgment, disentangle himself, and play hero—trying to kill twelve bird keepers with just seven stones, and possibly, two known unknowns.

The ends justifying the means through a lens of triggers and all that bullshit.

But neither of us are heroes, are we? And we don't know

how to do anything but re-affix the roles prescribed, over and over again. We don't know how to do anything but repeat the fucked up cycles of abuse we've suffered, do we? To punish ourselves and others for what was done to us, over and over again, in so many new, creative ways.

We're not heroes.

We're nothing more than a collection of horrible memories and prescribed ideas. They color everything we do, and working through the patterns to fix this is neither simple nor easy.

So, you can and probably should hate me. They can all hate me.

But not her. I'll die if she hates me.

I'm already—

BACK IN THE VENT, Alex, Diana, Olivia and Sebastian were making slow progress. There were just too many paths to travel down and too many unknowns. Olive had tried her best to lead the charge, but she was grasping in the dark for a thread she couldn't see.

Luckily, something slapped right into Olivia's face, directly into her forehead. She hadn't seen it coming and instantly let out a yelp.

"What?!" the trio behind her yelled out in near-perfect unison. Alex tried to push past Diana to attend to Olive; Diana was having none of that. Diana and Alex struggled against each other in an effort to both be the hero.

"Move your fat ass!" Alex barked at Diana as she started

hitting him with flat palms, slapping as children do, over and over again.

"Ow!" Olivia said, rubbing her forehead. She picked up the little robot and held it in her hands, sitting back on her rear.

"Knock it off, you two!" Sebastian growled and sharply turned to stare at them as best he could. Diana had put Alex into a chokehold, with her breast squarely in his unamused face. They froze in place, waiting for Sebastian to look away, so they could continue to pummel each other.

"What is it, Olive?" Sebastian asked, crawling closer behind the small woman. Olive wrinkled her nose and turned the robot over in her hands.

"I...I dunno..." Olive said with a confused look on her face. She passed it back to the young man, and he turned it over and over in his hands.

"This is from one of the Wards, you know—military things. Repairs people, machines, broken coffee makers," Sebastian muttered.

"How do ya know?" Olive asked as she picked up the pace again, knees clunking on the metal below her.

Diana pushed at Sebastian's back, urging him to move. Sebastian slapped her hand away. Alex shoved at Diana from behind, again complaining about her fat ass.

"The branding here, they solder it in, like a tattoo," Sebastian said matter-of-factly, staring at the numbers on the underside of the muted green and grey little machine.

His palms began to sweat, and he abruptly changed the topic.

"Is anyone hot right now?" Sebastian asked, pulling at the collar of his shirt, the small robot sitting inert in his free hand.

"Huh?" Olivia responded as she moved forward, confused by his question. The young man made a sour face and shoved the tiny robot into his shirt. It dug in painfully, but he felt like he had to keep it.

"I'm…really warm," Sebastian said as he trudged forward, beads of sweat rolling down his face.

"Why not divest your shirt, *Mark*?" asked Diana in a sardonic tone.

"That's not my name anymore," he corrected her, "I can't. I'm keeping the robot there."

"Robot?" Diana asked, scuttling forward to peek over Sebastian's shoulder. She grew distracted. Alex thwunked her rear again with a fist.

"Hey!"

Olivia looked down into a deep hole that had cropped up ahead of her and let out a noise of wonder. Her voice echoed against the metal. She whistled. That, too, reverberated down, down, down into the depths.

"Alrighty everybody…we gotta' go down here, I think. Here goes nothin'!" the little thing said as she jumped down.

Sebastian scooted over the edge and looked down where Olive had flung herself into the gaping hole in the floor. His large eyes widened as sweat trickled down his chin.

"She's…very brave," Sebastian said in surprise, Olivia's form disappearing into the darkness of the mammoth hole.

"You mad?" Alex chortled from behind Diana. Diana, ever graceful, slammed into Sebastian's back as the young man tried to hold onto the sides of the vents to keep from falling into the abyss.

"Why would I be mad? Stop pushing me!"

Diana wrapped her arms around Sebastian and cooed from behind his ear. His shoulders went stiff as she grinned.

"Because she's braver than you, pet," Diana said with a girlish giggle as Alex pinched her rear. Diana slapped at his hand, and the two continued to tussle, shoving Sebastian forward despite all his efforts.

"Glad you two are having...*fun*. Let's go," Sebastian said, swallowing hard. He jumped as Olive had.

Diana hovered at the edge, turned to say something to Alex, but was kicked down into the abyss by the blond war machine.

Alex wasn't counting on Diana's reach being so long, however. She snagged the end of his foot and dragged him down with her.

"Fuck—" he screamed as he hung onto the vent's lip by his fingers. Diana purposefully flailed. Alex dropped down after her.

"You and your fat ass!"

He could hear Diana's velvety laughter all the way down.

Beyond the scurrying pests came the ever-important, time-table-adjusted event that had loomed, seemingly as an afterthought. But for Tyr, it was a priority. A party, a ceremony, a meeting; Vellians and the like. More than that, it was a wedding. All roads lead to this one spot in time. It was Tyr's main focus.

Sadly for Tyr, his puppets were either wholly incompetent, the pests were far too clever, or a combination of both. Sadly for the pests, Tyr was not nearly as inept as Alex had made him seem. The party would continue.

Tyr's hubris alone demanded it, as did the Vellians.

Floria, the ambassador and princess of Vellia was decked out in glistening jewels dripping from her neck as if part of her skin. Skin that was deep blue with ripples of purple veins.

Her eyes were lemon yellow and reptilian. Her hair was the same color in long waves down to the small of her back.

Her dress trailed across the lavish ballroom, inkling over

pink and white marble. It was sage and seaweed green with glimmers of transparent film.

Floria was very human-looking for all intents and purposes, aside from the colors and interesting textures. She spoke the common tongue of the station, as she wanted diplomacy between the station and her people to run smoothly.

Or as smoothly as it could, between two alien species.

But there was absolutely nothing human about her. Not in the way she moved, not what she spoke about, not her thoughts, her feelings, or how she viewed others.

They were all beneath her, and she had the glory of her position to wield that fact. Not unlike Tyr, who was thinking similar thoughts, idling with a champagne glass filled with golden liquid at the moment.

Floria offered the expression of her species that was customary for thanks: a slight nod of the head with her palms open to the ceiling.

Tyr mimicked her expression and passed her a dainty glass of bubbling gold.

"How are you enjoying the music?" asked Tyr, his striking features disarming even the Vellian beauty. She sipped her golden drink and tilted her head bird-like.

"It is not usual. But it is pleasant," she said coldly with a sideways glance to the bustling orchestra.

Tyr clinked his glass with her own. She suffered a human smile that spread too taut across her teeth. Her species smiled to threaten, not please—or deceive—others.

"I always aim to be pleasant. Here's to our glorious partnership and ushering both our species to an alternative future," Tyr said, taking a sip of his own liquor.

Vellians and humans decked out in garish fineries danced upon the marbled floor. The violins whirled. Tyr flirted with a being who was incapable of flirting, but he interested her enough to entertain his movements.

"When will It arrive?" Floria asked, her collarbone shifting underneath her skin like a rod beneath plastic.

"Shortly, my dear fiancé," his words were wicked, even when sweet. "First, we must set the stakes…it will be a marvelous play."

The ceiling beyond their heads bled out in colors of blue and green, a scenery change that dotted down the walls in heavy dollops of digital-organic paint.

The ceiling blossomed into the painting Tyr was partial to—angels with clouds between their thighs and devils now ripping throats clean through.

Gold ushered up from the columns and gilded the lining of the walls in a baroque menagerie.

It was a mixing of styles he found both decadent and terrifying.

Floria lifted her free hand to the sky, pleased with this new ceiling. The dancers whirled, the music picked up, and Tyr finished up his golden drink.

"…and there will be no obstacles?" Floria asked, ending her sentence on a sound not unlike a bird's warble.

"No."

"He'll fold. For them," Tyr sipped more of his drink, "For them, he'll fold. He always does, in one way or another."

For the group in the vents, the fall had been farther than they expected, but the landing wasn't half as bad as they thought. They had landed in water.

Trudging through the darkness with water up to their waists—and up to Olivia's torso—they said nothing for a time.

"...the water's hot..." Olive said, wrinkling up her nose.

Alex pressed something on his chest. He lit up at the seams. Blue rippled over the clear water, just enough for them to see where they were going, as well as the ghostly outlines of each other.

"...what?" spat Alex, looking back at Olive. Olive stared at Sebastian.

Olivia moved around Sebastian in a wide circle and then

back towards the young man. Back and forth again, with Alex raising his brows to his hairline at her antics. Diana did much the same.

"Yer...makin' the water hot," Olive said, stalking towards Sebastian to snatch his hand. She winced and pulled away. She looked at her stinging palm and quirked a thin brow.

Sebastian said nothing, but he did stare at his hands.

"So...you have time powers," Alex reasoned, pointing at Olivia, "And you boil water," he pointed at Sebastian, "Good to know."

"Smart-ass," Sebastian said under his breath, then splashed Alex across the back with a swath of water.

"Hey! I don't know if I'm fucking waterproof!"

"You are, pet. Like mascara," Diana joked, nudging Alex with her shoulder. He stumbled and then pushed Diana into the water. She laughed, sputtered, then attempted to pull him down with her.

"We don't—hey. We don't have tha' time fer this...c'mon you two!" said Olive, chopping through the water.

Sebastian braced the bottom of his shirt with his hand and looked down his chest. Even the little medical robot was hot to the touch.

"What's with the fucking lake?" Alex asked, cutting ahead to end up on a tiled floor. The water had given way to a shore-line of laminate gridwork.

"There are wonders here," was all Sebastian said before he struck ahead of Alex to flip on a switch. Blue light bathed the room with a mechanical hum, then it turned yellow.

Old furniture, rotten from the moisture, filled the room. The tiles had warped below the water like a spatial distortion or a lake made from a glacier.

"Looks like a fucking surrealist nightmare," Alex said through clenched teeth, then swerved around a familiar busted couch. He made a motion for the door. It was locked.

He tried it again, but his brute force was somehow not enough to dislodge it.

"...you can't get it open, dear?" Diana asked, stumbling out of the water. She wicked the moisture from her dress and stooped to pull off her heels.

"...no. It's," Alex hesitated, then shot out his arm to bash at the couch nearest him. He felt his fake muscles scream, the graphene bones of his wrist ache, and his knuckles clunk.

"...I've been neutered. That royal shithead—"

"What? I thoughtcha' said you had—" Olive began, hopping onto the tiles. She wriggled the water off of her body.

"I do! It's—"

"You're cut off," Sebastian said, shifting to use his free hand to wrench at the door's handle, "....and without you to demolish everything in our path..."

"We're fucked, is what you're saying," Alex finished Sebastian's sentiments. Diana pouted. Olive let out a heavy sigh.

After a moment, Diana steeled herself, slid forward, and flung one of her high heels at the door. It flapped against the metal and dropped feebly with a dull thwunk.

"...what did you think that was going to do, Di?" asked Alex, rolling his eyes like Polly would.

Another heel slapped the door with a muted thud.

"I-I don't know, darling, but it made me feel better!"

THE TEAM THAT HAD spent their time screaming—shooting—and punching oceans of guards to death hadn't yet fully stopped their carnage. Vox had ended up doing more damage than Polly—who upon realizing she didn't have to put in the effort—lagged behind Henry.

Henry wrapped his arm around Polly's shoulders. The thick-browed man winced as a strange beeping noise pierced his ears.

"Eh, Poll. Whassat beepin'?" he asked the blonde woman, who shook her head, wincing as he had.

Vox wasn't paying attention to the shrill alarm, as she was angry enough to tear a hole in time and space itself.

"Can we, like, not...be this angry, or whatever?" Polly droned, still yet wincing.

"You would police my actions?!" Vox roared, staring back at the pale woman with fire in her eyes, "You will be silent," Vox said, spitting vitriol as she wheeled forward and kicked at a valve on the wall.

The beeping noise stopped.

"Hmm...is this the source?" Vox asked aloud. The beeping resounded, and so she did the only logical thing and struck the valve again with her serrated heel. Vox was dauntless.

"...Yer proper mad at that one, eh?" Henry said, gesturing at the valve. With one last smash, she broke the valve into thousands of tiny pieces. The petals of metal scattered to the floor. She ground them beneath her heels.

"...the noise stopped, or whatever..." Polly muttered.

Polly narrowed her eyes then grasped Henry's hand to walk him forwards. She shot him a look that spelled 'she's crazy,' but he hadn't read it. Henry had never been much of a reader.

A jeering alarm ricocheted around them. It was a shrill, impossible siren. A blood-red light bathed the hall.

"Like?! What did you do?!" Polly screeched at Vox, hands clutched to her ears as Henry tried to drag her onwards.

Vox held her head in her hands. She scanned the area, trying to pinpoint the sound.

"I am...not sure," Vox shouted over the sound of the wailing alarm.

"Well, like, make it stop, or whatever!" Polly screeched.

BACK AT THE PARTY, Tyr's perfect plans seemed to have been derailed by a slight slip of technical debt caused by none other than the songbird who couldn't sing.

"Sir, we have a problem," whispered a guard into Tyr's ear. The guard had caused him to stop dancing, which he was mutely annoyed at. Floria spindled away and continued her haptic movements.

Humans and Vellians didn't move the same. Tyr had spent months perfecting their awkward dance.

"Speak," Tyr motioned with his palm.

"...a valve broke. We need it for the flush." Tyr whirled around the unassuming guard and clutched him by the collar of his uniform. It was white, pure, perfect, but the gun at his side was dark chrome.

"You will fix this," he seethed. Floria caught his glance. Tyr slacked his grip.

"S-sir, it's old tech. It's going t-to take a while," Tyr's grip tightened, "it's-it's gonna take," Tyr constricted his grip once more and the guard grew silent.

"I need an inciting action—not that you'd understand what that even means, you insignificant maggot. Take all available pains to remedy the situation. I do not care what you must sacrifice for it. If you cannot do this, I will have no choice but to send a known unknown of his genus. This, I would like to avoid. Do we have an understanding?" Tyr hissed through his teeth.

The guard in white nodded violently, choked by the collar.

Tyr pulled away, leaving the guard to shake like a leaf. Tyr met Floria's outstretched fingers and began their dance yet again.

"Yes...sir..." the guard said, twisting back to leave the lavish ballroom.

The guard passed by a newly placed indigo swath of fabric. The entire room was set around this one violent blue. Hesitating, the guard finally left.

"Is everything agreeable?" Floria asked, sweeping around in a dance, tethered by the gravity of Tyr's hand.

"All is going according to plan, my dear," he replied, dipping the Vellian beauty back over the canvas of blue, "I just need to find...the right amount of pressure," he hummed.

Floria twisted away, yet Tyr caught her fingers in his own to pull her back into an embrace. She studied what she could see of his face with her striking yellow eyes.

He gave her nothing in his glance.

ALEX, SEBASTIAN, Diana, and Olive were still stuck on their leg of the journey. The door beyond the strange surrealist lake was not budging. At this point, Alex had the bright idea to bash his fists against it, but Sebastian pushed him aside.

Taking the small robot from his shirt, Sebastian put it in Alex's hands, who stared at it dumbly.

"...why are you giving me this glorified toaster?" Alex asked, turning it over in his hands, "it's hot as fuck...shit," Alex said, tossing it into the air.

"It's important. See if you can hook up to it," Sebastian said, sweat still yet dripping down his face.

"How the fuck do you know it's important?" Alex spat.

"I just do," Sebastian muttered before moving to press his hands to the door. He closed his eyes and felt the metal heat up beneath his fingers.

"...are you tryna' use The Force?" asked Olivia with a devilish little smile. Alex cackled.

"That's a good one, Liv," the blond snorted. Diana smiled behind her fingers, a giggle escaping her.

"You're all a bunch of…children," Sebastian said, trying to exert more effort into the door. He pressed, the metal grew warm.

"You trying to use your 'magic touch' to melt the metal?" Alex asked, wiggling his fingers. Sebastian shot daggers at Alex. The blond's smile was criminal.

"Please, don't remind me."

"Why not? Why not remind you?" Alex asked with a razored grin. Al whirled the small robot into the air and settled it in his palms. Another toss and Sebastian was steadily growing more irate.

"You can't keep punishing me, Al," Sebastian responded, the metal growing hot under his fingers.

"I sure can, and you're going to take it, like a good bo—"

"Children, children," Diana piped up, holding out her hands in an attempt to keep the peace.

"Hey, it's doin' something—" Olive started up, pointing at the door, but it was lost to Alex's verbal gouging.

"…you really thought you were God's Gift—What was it that you used to say?" Alex asked, the words lush in his mouth. The small robot spun in the air once more.

"Al, I'm warning you," Sebastian hissed. A bead of sweat dripped down his hairline to his jaw.

"Warning me? Me, of all people, you're going to fuckin' warn?" The small robot dropped to the floor with a dead thud as Alex shot forward to rip Sebastian from the door.

"You used to say that I was lucky because you were fond of me. You, the head of our branch of fuckery. That it was you, so very, very powerful, and not someone else. That you never started something you couldn't finish," Alex continued, his voice now booming across the tiled walls.

"...but you didn't fucking finish it. Did you, Mark?" Alex was made of acid.

"You were always so easily frightened, little bird," Sebastian said softly, "I get it. You're not strong now, and you're worried about your friends. But dredging up the past is—" Sebastian paused. Olive was looking at him. He quirked an inexpressive brow. She gave him a small nod.

Sebastian placed both hands on the door, bracing himself on the metal.

"Keep going," Sebastian said, "I can do this, but you have to keep at it—"

"Oh, I'll keep at it alright," Alex said, teeth grit, jaw clenched. He rolled up his sleeves in a show of machismo. Sebastian held his breath. He knew what was coming.

It wasn't a fist to the face, but it'd hurt like one.

"The reason you're trying to climb the fucking ladder here is the same reason you climbed it before," Alex snarled, eyes alight with the rage of a supernova.

"You love power. You love control. You are exactly the type of fucking garbage-person I hate most," Alex bulleted his words out in rapid-fire.

Sebastian braced his hands more firmly on the door but never let his eyes wander from Alex's neon blue gaze.

"Because you don't 'give' anything, Markov," the blond gestured, shoulders taut and fists clenched, "You never gave anyone anything. You wouldn't even give me the dignity of telling me what you really are," Alex's fists were shaking.

The wound had never healed. Maybe it never would.

"And what is it that I am, Alexei?" Sebastian hissed, his fingers tingling on the metal of the door. It began to change color from drab gray to humming orange.

"Look...it's—" Olive was silenced.

"An addict. A predator. If it's not sex, it's power. If it's not power, it's control. Alcohol was always an excuse to be yourself. You power grabbing, money loving, selfish, ignorant, control-freak piece of shit!"

"And what of you, Alexei?!" spat Sebastian, the metal under his palms blossoming in searing orange.

"You get off on the same exact thing!" Sebastian roared, finally brought to anger enough that his own jaw clenched. Alex was about to snap back, but the young man continued, barreling over the synth's words with his own daggered language.

"You kill not because you have to, but because it gets your dick hard." Silence.

"You're a being of pure, unadulterated chaos! You love to wound and be wounded. It's war. It's all the same thing," Sebastian only paused long enough to look at the door as it turned white-hot. Metal dripped down his fingers and wrists like lava. It burned him no longer.

"How you ever got on with Olivia, sweet, kind Olivia, is beyond me—" The metal poured down his wrists as the door bled chrome.

"Don't you bring her into this, you witless fuck—"

"I didn't break you Alexei! Don't you understand?! You were already broken!" Alex's fist crashed into Sebastian's skull with a sickening thud.

As the pair fought against each other, the hole Sebastian had made seared open further. The hallway beyond them was pitch black aside from a few red dots of light. None of them seemed to notice.

Alex pinned Sebastian at the wrists with one hand and had taken to pounding his skull in.

"Pet, pet stop! Stop!" Diana yelled, dashing forward on bare feet to snatch Alex's arm. He knocked her away. She tripped over the small robot on the floor. Olivia moved to Diana's side and helped her stand.

"Are you ok?" Olivia asked.

"Yes, yes dear. I'm *fine*. But we have to stop them," Diana trailed off. Olivia made no movement besides helping Diana.

The sound of metal pummeling flesh repeated like a sickening drumbeat until Sebastian turned the heat up and melted the plasticine skin from Alex's hands. It dripped down the blond synth's metal digits and flicked into the air with each visceral smash.

"You absolute piece of shit!" roared the war machine.

Olive watched them fight, her hands hanging limply at her sides. Her thin brows raised up. Her sparse eyelashes fluttered. She inhaled deeply. Felt the wet clothes on her skin.

She knew where all this came from. They needed to burn the wound to close it. They had to set it on actual fire.

"Stop! You're going to kill him, darling. Stop!" Diana fumbled on her still yet twisted ankle and finding it throbbing, clung uselessly to Olive's shoulder.

"You melted my—" another punch landed, and this time it was stronger than the last, "motherfucking hands!"

Olivia inhaled and watched the blood fly. A fleck crested her cheek. Olive dotted it with her fingers. She pulled her hand back to look. Violet in all this violence, where she'd expected red.

"You took everything from me! I'd see your goddamn face!" Another punch landed, but Sebastian managed to break free and brace his hand on the synth's jeering arm. Alex tore away just as his sleeve started to sizzle.

The red dots lingered in the door-frame. Diana heard a distant mechanical sound.

"Darlings—"

"I'd see your face, and feel like I was dying! Do you understand, Markov?! Do you have any idea what I sacrificed just to get to sit at your fucking table? Do you have any idea what I gave you—" Sebastian managed to scramble away as Alex grew increasingly unstable.

Alex's breathing grew shallow, his fake heart beat like a terrified bird in a metal cage.

"...any idea...any idea...what I really wanted..." Alex crumpled to his knees, wrapping his hands around his ears. He coddled his head as he bent to the floor, pale hair strewn feather-like.

"Then tell me already." Sebastian stuttered, mouth twisted acidly. His palms were planted on the tiles. His face was busted. His nose was practically shattered. He'd have more than a bruise from this, yet the pain felt as nothing.

"I wanted. I..." Alex's face rose up, stained with blue. He couldn't look Sebastian in the eyes. He couldn't look anyone in the eyes.

"You wanted to be the person you never got to be," Olivia's childish phrasings were dashed to the rocks, "Not the one people made you into."

Alex said nothing.

Sebastian lightly touched his broken face with burning fingers in some vain attempt to fix the damage by himself. He stopped; his hands were coated violet. Disbelief flashed in his eyes. Olive's sentence reclaimed his focus.

"I'm...missing something, aren't I?" Sebastian muttered, "what am I not seeing? What...didn't I hear?" Sebastian searched the memories that had been so easily given to him before.

It was harder now than it had ever been, because he wasn't simply witnessing memory fragments. He was scanning for something. Sebastian—Markov—had to look at who he'd truly been.

The first time the two men met, the chatter around them was mindless. Heavy accents floated in the air like tethered mobiles. They were set apart, drinking beer, but the gravitation was visible. Alexei was a new recruit, but recognized by others. Markov had been told he was born into the group.

Yet he had never seen him before. This meeting was meant to change that, because apparently the unknown one had talent.

Alex was wearing a long-sleeved crew-neck in the summer. Markov remembered the color—Alex's permanent indigo. He also remembered the shorter man being very nervous, fiddling with the tableware.

"I'm happy to finally meet you face to face—sorry, fuck. That's stupid, wait. Let me start again."

Start again, he did. Several times, actually, and in several different languages.

As the meeting went on, Alex grew less nervous and Markov grew more intrigued.

"....and you're the one who took them all down? All of them?" Markov asked, followed by a gulp of beer.

"I am," Alex replied, giving Markov a modest smile before sipping his own beer.

The taller man rubbed his hand over his mouth and took in the shorter man's features. The shorter man fidgeted with a fork, but looked at Markov intensely.

"Do you doubt me?" Alex asked, his feline brow raising. He jerked his head around to look for someone. "Boris," the blond crooned, wagging the fork to his palm like a fidget.

Markov watched Alex's ministrations with a curious smile. The fellow Markov liked least rounded the table, smelling of strong cigars.

"Little bird calls, and I answer. I do like to hear you sing," the man said with a deep, hearty laugh. Boris reached for Alex's idle beer mug. Alex let him take it. Boris rested his other hand on the table as he chugged it down. Alex leaned back in his seat and tapped the fork on the table's edge like a metronome.

"Care to regale Mark here with my fables?" the blond preened, no longer nervous.

"Mark…" Markov was nearly speechless. Alex's confidence had come on like a grenade. Where was the nervous, fidgeting, awkward man of before?

"Aha, of course—" In an instant, Alex jammed his fork into the meat of Boris' hand, halting the beer-thief's words.

Markov was now actually speechless, while Boris was pouring out broken swears in every single color.

"If you remember what I'm capable of, you'll remember not to fucking call me 'little bird' ever again."

"Is it a nickname?" Markov asked Alex, ignoring Boris altogether, who attempted to remove the fork but only succeeded at screaming and bleeding.

Alex gave Mark a mute smile.

"No," the blond said, taking back his mug of beer and downing a deep sip, "it's a genre. Or, you know what, never mind. I don't think you'd get it."

This one would go on to do great things. That's what Sebastian remembered. He remembered being Markov and wanting to shape that greatness.

He remembered that look in Alex's eyes, before the fork, and the smile that came after.

Sebastian tried to focus. There was a black spot in all he saw; an ignored thing, an idea, a concept threaded on itself like a twisted cord. Something only Alex could loop around his wrists and orchestrate.

Sebastian couldn't see it clearly.

As Alex became his machine of war, Markov never knew

where all the anger came from. Never knew why he enjoyed it so much. He never understood the razor-edged smile.

Players that had their hands in business Alex didn't look fondly on dropped like shell casings. If they weren't pushed out, they were replaced or went missing. Markov had noticed this but had disregarded it.

Encouraged it, even, as he encouraged Alex to rise to where he knew he could be. If that was his path to greatness, that's what it was. He also had no love for men like Boris and certainly no love for what they did.

There were lines in the sand that they both agreed should not be crossed.

However, it was Alex that proposed what these lines were. It was Alex who had placed that idea in his head, through his warm ear, from his trembling mouth. It had been Alex that made his position painfully clear in their organization while pinned below the taller man, and yet he had held the strings around Markov's throat the entire time.

He had never been a prey animal.

Sebastian thought on this, eyes flicking over Alex's fractured expression.

"You used me," Sebastian seethed, but hesitated, "No, that's—"

He remembered Alex's face after their first tryste, years after the fork incident.

"This is…dangerous," Alex said as he lit up a cigarette. Smoke withered from the blond's mouth and found its way up to the ceiling. It spiraled like a swirling nebula. Alex pulled the sheets onto his lap. He gave Markov a hesitant smile.

Alex didn't sit very close to Markov, but he did reach across the vast expanse between them to give him a cigarette.

"Yes, but I'm sure we can handle it," Markov took the cigarette.

"Can you?" asked the blond, giving the other man a cautious look. The smoke orbited his face and broke to flit through the window.

Markov took the chance to run his fingers down the blond's spine, skipping over the eyes on his back to grasp his side and reel him closer. Alex gave him that and faced the other man, his cigarette dangling between his lips. "Don't make me regret giving you things," Alex gave Markov a warning with smoke blown in his face. "It's just a cigarette," Markov took it literally.

"God, you're fucking ignorant," Alex gave him a dry smile before leaning to tap ash in his pink yarrow ashtray, "...and you're avoiding it."

"Avoiding what?" Markov asked, rummaging for a lighter by the end-table. Markov twisted, jerked open the drawer, knocked over the tiny potted plant on top of it, and soured. Finding nothing, Markov turned back to Alex, only to receive a Bic lighter placed in his palm.

"The genre...there's a reason I'm here, and I do what I do, so I'm asking you not to make me regret giving you—" Markov obviously didn't understand this answer because he plucked the cigarette from between Al's lips and stole his words with a blistering kiss.

Sebastian held his head, taking in just a scrap of memory. The parts that held the pieces he had yet to put together, even after all this time and all this space, grew clear.

"Little bird. The eyes. A genre. Boris and his trade. The van joke. Lines in the sand. The bar. Your plans, to do something..." the words spilled from Sebastian's lips. The lips that now curdled, a grimace fit for horrors he had never thought on, done to a man he had never thought to ask about them.

He had ignored the genre.

"...something awesome..." Sebastian closed his eyes, "which you did. You pulled it off," he whispered, "there would be no more caught and kept little birds with clipped wings in your city for as long as you lived."

"Ya' get it now," Olive chirped, a hand on her hip.

"How did you know?" Sebastian asked, flicking his eyes to her face.

"I'm tha' clever one, doncha' know?" Olivia snorted.

"I'm not sure I get it, dear..." Diana protested as she swiveled on her wounded ankle, "darlings...why do I feel that you've left me out?" she pouted. Alex locked eyes with Diana and shook his head, a soft gesture.

"Saying it makes it real," the blond hesitated, "...I can't."

"It's alright, dear," Diana hummed, stooping awkwardly to pick up the medical robot from the floor. She turned it around to examine the underside. After a few moments, her previous pout became something solemn.

Then, her expression became the one she knew to be her truest but showed others rarely—overwhelmed, yet hardly graceful.

"...I think I understand, a little. Tyr-things, and men who never give, and all that dreadfulness," Diana knit her brows as she spoke, "...what was it I said before? 'What monsters they leave out'? Oh—" Diana paused, standing perfectly still.

Alex looked away instinctively, prey-like and raw from a psychic wound that had never healed.

"...we've subverted that story, haven't we? Someone gave Dolores dear a pistol along the way...well, you weren't there to hear that, anyway, dear..." Diana's sentence drifted like feathers through the air, as did her focus.

"Yes and no. I took the pistol by force," Alex hissed, still not looking at Diana. Diana looked up from the small robot and at the blond's profile. Perhaps seeing him, truly, for the first time. Then, her gaze traveled to the melted doorway. A trio of red dots greeted her; small, distant.

"Hmm…darlings—"

"Your face…looks fucking horrible," Alex said to Sebastian, abruptly changing the topic.

"I'm sorry," Sebastian said, low in the throat. He stood and stepped towards the synth, who scuttled back just as quickly.

"I'm…so sorry."

"Darlings, I'm very proud of you for hashing this all out, but I fear we've overstayed our—"

"I'm sorry," Sebastian had given many apologies in the last few moments.

"...that was a lifetime ago. And you're right," Alex paused, his fake heart beating wildly in his chest, "I can't keep punishing you for a dumb mistake. Or for shit you're too dumb to figure out on your own."

"I think wrecking your face is enough. Now you look like human salami," Alex said with a muted smile, as the older man in a young man's body stepped away.

"Is it really that bad?" Sebastian asked. Alex hesitated to give him a laugh, but he did. He gave, and really hoped he wouldn't regret it.

"Sort of—" Alex was cut off by Diana.

"Boy—er—Pet. Use the small green 'thing.' But we must leave now," Diana said in soft words, placing the robot in Sebastian's hands, who stared at it quizzically.

"Why do we gotta' leave 'now'?" asked Olive. She was now holding Alex's metallic skeletal hand far too tightly.

"I saw red dots, darling, and we all know what that means," Diana said with a flat expression on her face.

Sebastian pressed a button on the bottom of the robot, but it refused to turn on.

"Let me try," Alex said, plugging himself into the back of the small machine. It whirled to life and trilled before it began to fix the damage he had done. Green light shimmered over Sebastian's features; his skin tingled and was numbed.

"...red dots?" Alex asked, still plugged into the machine. He pulled it forwards as he walked to look beyond the door. Sebastian staggered behind him.

"Again?" Olive groaned, losing Alex's hand.

"Really? Really. We have to fucking do this right now?" Alex added.

Diana pulled the small gun from between her breasts and motioned to the others.

"Get ready, dears. Something's comi—" A deafening scream filled the room, knocking everyone save Sebastian to the floor.

The door frame buckled under the pressure. The medical robot slammed into the far wall with a hollow thwump and dropped into the water.

"Ah fack. Why're you lot on tha' ground?" Henry had apparently barreled into the room, followed by Polly.

"Guys!" Olive chirped, rising up off her knees. As her head was bowed, she lingered to look behind herself at the medical bot twirling uselessly in the water.

"Pepto!" Henry started but was caught off guard by Sebastian's destroyed face. "Oy, mate...what 'appened t'ya face?" Henry asked as the sound of metal tearing and clanking ripped through the air.

Sebastian rolled his eyes but didn't bother answering him. Instead, he reached out a hand to Alex.

"Thanks...Sebastian," the blond said, taking the other man's hand and using it to stand. Alex accepted the peace offering and hoped it wasn't temporary.

"Hey, Erica," Alex said softly. Henry would have replied but was stampeded by a limping Diana. She smothered Henry in a crushing embrace.

"Mate! Agh—Di, yer cuttin' off m'oxygen is wh—"

Polly stormed through the door, her floral dress covered in blood, "...like, we need...to run now, or whatever. She won't be able to hold it off forever." Polly looked back to see Diana cloistering Henry. She pressed herself between them in an attempt to stop it.

Sadly for her, Diana took to hugging the poor girl to death as well.

"Already ahead of ya'!" Olive said, splashing into the water with elongated strides.

Henry and Polly managed to wrestle free from Diana's stranglehold, but she simply went on to her next victim.

"Proud of you, darling," Diana cooed, hugging Sebastian to her chest. He grimaced into her honey-colored skin as she choked him

"You don't even know what any of that was about!" Sebastian grumbled into her breasts.

"Still proud of you!" Diana chortled and constricted Sebastian's airflow.

"You shouldn't be too proud. It only took him a couple fuckin' thousand years," Alex said with a sneer, but it melted when he saw just how royally fucked Sebastian's face was.

"I am—actually—really. Fucking. Sorry. About the face," Alex said, nodding with each word.

"You mean it? You're actually, really, fucking, sorry?" Sebastian parroted his nods dramatically, sarcasm poisoning his mimicry.

"Well, yeah—" Alex snorted.

Olive dredged herself up to where the small robot fell and picked it up with her hands. Placing it under her arm, she used her free hand to bang her fist on the wall, making a heavy sound. She clashed her fist against the panel beside it. This time, the sound was hollow.

"Henry, I need yer help!" Olive shouted, which prompted Henry to look at her.

A metallic crashing sound exploded beyond the doorway. A sonic scream followed soon after, with Polly nowhere to be seen. Henry would not be making his maiden voyage across the lake.

"Poll, no—Gawdammnit woman…Vox, if you n' barbie don't wanna get killed—" Henry bellowed through the doorway between cupped hands.

"I know, yes," Vox said as she hustled through. Polly, however, continued her assault on whatever it was she was fighting.

Back at the water, Olive roared in frustration and used the small medical bot to bludgeon the panel she had found. It popped open. Olive primed her arm to fling the small robot now that she was done with it.

Diana limped through the water to rescue the medical bot from Olive's clutches.

"Don't just throw it away, darling! We have injured here," Diana chastised. Olive grimaced at her.

Sebastian sighed and moved his flat palm down the entire length of his face. "This truly is hell, isn't it?" Sebastian grumbled.

"Yes," Vox said as she passed him, narrowing her eyes at the body of water now in front of her, "…why is there a lake here?" Vox asked.

"Because it's fucking hell," Alex offered, which made Vox

grit her teeth.

Alex snagged Sebastian's arm and dragged him through the water. He pulled up beside Diana and snapped his reel into the medical bot. It was still functional.

"Don't say I never did nothin' for you, Bastian," Alex spat.

"Oh," Sebastian squinted, "Oh, I do not like that nickname."

"Tough shit."

"Boys! Please!" Diana groaned.

Olive, ever the problem solver, ripped open the panel she'd bashed at. She swiped her palm over an unassuming clear panel.

"It's…an elevator," Olive stammered out, hazel eyes flickering over the transparent display.

"Can you get it working, princess?" Alex asked.

"No, I need—"

"Roight," Henry rounded the group and rolled up his sleeves, rubbing his hands together. His palms began to tingle with small lines of light.

"We're in water, you *simpleton*," Vox hissed. His charged palms fizzled out, as did his expression.

"Alright, fuck, let's get this show on the road. Percy, get your dumb ass back here!" Alex screamed, calling her by her original name. He slammed his fist into the panel. It didn't do anything.

Elsewhere, the bottle-blonde banshee booked it towards the door. The sound that came after her was worse than her own powerful screams, and the thing that made it was far worse than anything they could have ever imagined.

It gnashed. Its frame was made of bone, graphene, and plasticine. Strips of what looked to be like flesh clung to it. It was an organic machine, a hybrid, blown apart and spindled on arachnid legs. It was a hellish monstrosity of machine and human parts. Its fat central body gyrated against its frame, pulsing with blue fluid. Three red dots were situated in a swivel, just as the other automaton had been. It squelched and smelled of death.

"Oh holy fuck…" Alex gawked, lunging to tear Olivia, Diana, and Sebastian away from the panel.

Henry sprinted to Polly, snagged her by the waist, and nearly peeled out on the tiles but managed to bolt back around. Vox deftly side-stepped the attack.

Searing heat scoured the tiles and burned up in a red line towards the elevator. The panel exploded in a beam of light. An old metal door shuttered open. A thick black cord extended below.

There was no elevator car in sight.

"Come on!" Olive shouted as she leapt from Alex's grip and launched through the opening.

Henry flung Polly into the opening and joined her shortly after. Vox pulled Diana to her body and jettisoned towards the elevator, with the femme fatale screaming the entire way down.

"We need to buy them some time," Alex hissed under his breath. Sebastian pulled away from Alex, nodding.

The two men looked at the bulbous, pus-seeping monstrosity on its mechanical arachnid limbs and grimaced in unison.

This wasn't going to be simple, nor would it be easy.

"...MAN, I knew he was a sick fuck, but I didn't think he was this demented..." Alex muttered, gawking at the gyrating, mechanically gored beast.

"Yes," Sebastian paused, mouth hanging open, "Well," he tilted his head slightly, "It seems terrorizing us might just be his main goal, after all. But why not just kill us, outright?"

Alex sized up their opposition. It was horribly fast yet incredibly inefficient. It hobbled towards them, then jagged swiftly, trying to cleave both men in two. It was like a tumor on legs, spilling bile with each movement.

"You're saying he's after somethin' else?" Alex asked, lurching out of the way of one of its skewers, dragging Sebastian with him.

"I'm saying there are far easier ways to deal with pests— shit!" Sebastian belted out as Alex tore him out of harm's way yet again. The pair stumbled.

Alex maneuvered to stand in front of Sebastian as though the war machine without his superpowers could threaten their enemy by glaring at it.

"So, blondie. How do you propose to get us out of this situation?" Sebastian paused, "Preferably alive."

"I—"

The creature above them thundered out a horrific mechanical roar and reeled towards them.

"Oh fuck—" Alex belted out and launched to the side. Sebastian scrambled after him and lept adjacent to his shoulder.

A turret in metal pushed through the creature's skin, parting the flesh in a wound. One of its thin black legs stabbed at Alex and cracked the tile ahead of him like an eggshell.

In a moment of genius or stupidity, Alex scooped up the small medical robot off the ground as he ran, jacked his cord into its side, and started pressing its buttons.

"Maybe I can get on the network and shut it the fuck down," Alex blurted out as the pair of men side-stepped when the beast tried to puncture them in two. Alex smashed his fingers in a familiar—stupid—pattern.

"It's. Alex. Alex! It's not Street Fighter. Al—No. You're. You're doing it wrong. Throw it. Throw it to me!" Sebastian yelled.

"*Fine!*" Alex spat as he tossed the medical bot behind himself. Sebastian scrambled forward to catch it.

The mechanical beast's leg came down above them. Alex bolted to avoid being crushed to death. Sebastian jerked after him and scuttled, continuing to bash the buttons in no discernible pattern.

"We're playing hot potato with this thing. This is fucking stupid!" Alex barked as Sebastian chased after him, fumbling to make sure he didn't disconnect from the smaller robot. "And you're just doing," the monster's turret hummed to attention, "what I was doing! Do you even know how to work that thi—"

Pain shot through Alex's port.

He felt like every single synapse was on fire. His blood felt like acid. It bit the graphene bones and flayed through the crafted muscles. He felt like he was dissolving in a vat of his own juices.

"Got it. You're on the network…"

"Agh—fuck," the blond groaned.

Sebastian shot him a glance.

"Alex?"

The seams of Alex's shell were alight with the color of war, the color of poppies, of blood, of the nebula nearest them, of pain, and of the trick for men. The color crackled through the inked story on his skin and burned in neon light.

"Al?"

Alex screamed the dual-toned sound of an exploding star.

"Alex, s-snap out of it!" Sebastian hissed, lunging to snatch Alex's arm, but the synth was writhing against himself hard enough to tear his muscles. Sebastian staggered back, hand to his mouth.

The turret of the armatron whirled, seizing impossible power in a glory of blue light.

"F —" a series of glitched syllables sparked from Alex's mouth. His neck nearly snapped from the force that was lighting tremors through his shell. His bones were breaking apart. This would be how he died. He'd die. He was dying.

"Alex!"

The small robot in Sebastian's arms caved in on itself. Sebastian dropped it to the floor like a heavy stone. It scuttled towards the blond, insect-like.

"Alexei!" Sebastian ripped towards the blond but stumbled to the floor as the beast above them tried to puncture him through the middle. It missed, veering closer to the malfunctioning war machine as if magnetized.

"Mark—" Alex shot his arm out to reach for Sebastian, his entire arm shaking.

A searing pain shot through Al's head as the small medical robot latched to his body and melted into his skin. The sage artifice cleaved around him and scaffolded chrome up his body.

The legs of the armatron beast began to buckle. It stumbled as one of them dislodged and careened towards the blond. Then, it attached itself, just like the smaller robot had.

Alex was a black hole siphoning every single piece of unthinking, unfeeling metal in the room.

"M-Mark...what's—"

Sebastian had one hand over his mouth as he watched the armatron tear itself apart. It staggered towards them both. Its turret was still primed to fire in a glow of blue light. It washed over their features, then died, as it congealed over Alex's body.

WHO ARE YOU, a voice resounded in his metal skull.

"A—Alex. G-get the fuck out of my head!" The synth screamed and shrunk to his knees. Another piece of the giant beast unhinged itself and smashed into his body with a wet thud.

He consumed it all. Or rather, it consumed him.

The armatron finally exploded in pieces of flesh, wiring, and circuitry and skittered across the floor towards the blond, leaving a trail of sick on the tiles below.

A large shard of metal stopped just short of cleaving Sebastian in two. The metal hummed as Sebastian stared at it.

"This...this is crazy..." Sebastian breathed out, his inexpressive brows pitching painfully.

"What did you do?!" Alex screamed as chrome ink submerged his face. Sebastian was silent, eyes wide as if watching the very end of the world unfold before him.

The piece of metal hovering in front of Sebastian scraped towards Alex, who struck out his hand to stop it from smashing through his own body.

It folded over his hand and crushed around his wrist, crawling up his arm like a parasite.

"Stop!" half-screamed the blond, but his scream was deafened in a film of metal.

Alex had no need to breathe, but now he felt like he was starved of oxygen. He was drowning in black waters. He was going to die. He was dying. It wanted to devour him. He was being eaten alive. He was going to die.

"No...Alex!" Sebastian surged forward and burned through the liquid metal of his once-paramour's face, tearing it from his eyes uselessly.

Alex could now hear Olive shouting.

He saw Vox from the corner of his eye running forward, with Olive lagging behind her. They had climbed out of the elevator shaft.

Each one of them stood there while metal encased his body, mouths open. Sebastian gave everything he had to pull the blond free. His arms were covered in flames, and still, it was not enough.

A mechanical cord burst through a wall and jacked into Alex's body, right in the back of his head. The sound of electricity blitzed from inside his skull.

"Alex!" Olive screamed and held up her hands to try to stop time as she had before. The liquid metal stopped for but a moment, jagged in the air as if scratched with a pen, and then resumed its path.

Polly let out a deafening scream. The metal bent around her soundwave like water and javelined through Alex's torso.

The cable at Alex's neck lifted him into the air, and another cable shot out to attach to his shell. He was soon covered in mechanical black ivy.

Alex's stricken hand came up to clench the cord at his neck in a shaking fist. Blue liquid pooled from the back of his head. He managed to rip the cord out with a sickening sound, but another took its place.

"FUCK. OFF!" he bellowed from the metal bubble over his mouth.

As metal slipped over his face in rivers, he looked down to see Olive crying and Diana covering the little pixie's eyes with her hand. Polly was still trying to blast apart moving pieces. Sebastian was petrified in place with chrome dripping from his smoldering fingertips.

Vox was ripping cables out of the wall as soon as they cropped up, but there were too many of them. Henry was frozen in place, vague electricity jolting up his arms with no-where to go. Stupefied, he could do nothing.

USE IT.

"What the fuck does that *mean*?!" Alex screeched as he was raised higher into the air. Black cables clasped around his neck, squeezed and bolted through his mouth. He was being eaten alive.

In that moment, Alex had a thought—

YES.

If he was strong enough.

YES.

Could he overpower this?

YES.

If it wanted him this badly…could he manipulate it?

YES.

He wasn't who he used to be, but he had done a job like this so very long ago. He remembered. The red-painted lips, the calling card, the repeat job, the little bird, pecking out the eyes of bird keepers—

YES.

The ship shook and tilted on its axis. He had thrown off the ship's entire rotation. The walls were seething black liquid, dripping towards the synth encased and no longer fighting it.

WHO ARE YOU?

Alex's shell was gently lowered to the floor, lifeless like a mobile of flickering pale stars inside the black void of a galaxy.

Olive ran towards Alex and wrapped her arms around his chrome-covered body. It had hardened, but she still dug at it with her fingers.

Henry was trying to rip him free as he came down as well, but there was no use.

"Don't," Sebastian finally said. The others looked at him, except for Diana, who cursed at Sebastian in words from a different time.

Alex knew Diana was berating Sebastian, but he didn't know what she was saying.

He couldn't see her or hear her, but he could sense her. Not as heat, not as a schematic, not as a read-out. As *Her*. She, the matron, the mother-figure, the femme fatale, the bar-owner, the friend, the smiling devil with a snake on her shoulder, whose truest emotion was graceful overwhelm.

As Alex touched down, the chrome began to take on different colors. He drew up his hand as if passing through quicksand to stare at his fingers, not truly seeing them.

He could sense them in energy, memory, light, heat, and emotions.

"I'm…"

"…t-there you are…" Olivia murmured into his metal flesh, which soon turned to the shade it had been before.
The clothes repainted themselves as if they'd never been touched.

"I—I don't understand," Alex stammered out, "…how am I supposed to answer that fucking question?"

Olive shut her eyes tightly and held on. For that was all she could do, and the only answer she could give him, to a question she hadn't heard.

ALEX, AT THIS JUNCTURE, was still grappling with all that had transpired. Before being eaten by metal, and all that came after. He didn't understand, though he'd been paying attention. Well, at least he thought he had.

But this? He felt that all he'd done was let terrible things happen to him so that he could dish it out in worse colors. And against whom, exactly? Tyr?

Was Tyr genuinely the biggest threat they were facing? Alex wasn't so sure about that anymore, and that idea soured his expression. As Olive held fast to his side, he looked down at her and felt the warmth of her flickering star.

"We're...stuck. I'm. I'm stuck," his words pushed through his throat like once-wilted leaves.

"Ya' head get tossed n' all?" Henry responded in Olive's stead.

"It's fine...I'm fine, Henrietta. Erica. Heniffer. Herica,"

Alex said, followed by a stunted laugh.

Olive looked up at Alex's face. He scanned her face all the same, and then glanced at Henry, who was now hovering. He browsed through his would-be army, one by one, witnessing them as a unit.

Witnessing them as pieces to a puzzle.

Vox approached his side and placed a hand on his shoulder. He flinched. Polly was—as always—lost in space, but she pried her deep brown eyes to rest on his baby blues.

Diana was continuing to berate Sebastian, but Sebastian wasn't paying attention to her.

Sebastian stalked forward and grabbed Alex's face by the chin, looking into his eyes. Sebastian turned his head around, peering at it from every possible angle.

"S-stop mothering over me, you guys. You're fucking hovering," Alex spat.

"Sorry mate, ya' jus' had us scared an' all…" Henry replied, stepped back, and was now the current brunt of Diana's tirade.

"How could you just leave him here?! I kept trying to get us to go up, and you were just all, 'Nope, mate's got it covered.' What's wrong with you, you pathetic excuse for a man?!" Diana bellowed at Henry.

"I tried to go back." Olive said, pulling from Alex's chest to take his hand. It was sticky to the touch, and when she pulled it away, translucent blue fluid created a long string between her palm.

"…gross," Olive said, "what the heck is this stuff?"

"No fucking clue," Alex replied.

"Yes, but you're barely five feet tall! How could you climb?!" Diana was now frothing, "Henry's as tall as a mountain! Aren't you darling?! He could've climbed up!"

Vox tightened her grip on Alex's shoulder. Her mouth kept

opening, but she wasn't speaking. Alex locked eyes with the tall synth woman.

"What? Tell me," Alex asked, narrowing his eyes, "Vox, tell me."

"...it's a gift," Vox finally broke her silence.

Polly crossed her arms at this. This was far beyond her and probably beyond Henry, who was now prying at the back of Alex's head.

"A gift? From who?—Ow, Erica, cut the shit," Alex said, twisting to prevent Henry from prodding at his skull.

"Mate," Henry said, running his thumb over the blond's neck. Alex swatted Henry's hand away.

"When I was stuck in that bubble of black shit, something spoke to me. Asked me what I was. So who the fuck is it, and what do you mean by 'gift,' Vox?" Vox said nothing.

Henry snatched Alex by the shoulder and twisted him around, "Mate!" Henry insisted, shaking the now clearly pissed-off synth.

"What?!"

"It's...gone."

Sebastian rounded Alex and pushed Henry out of the way, scouring Alex's neck with his warmed fingers.

"He's right...the port is—" Sebastian's sentence was cut off.

"It's a gift," Vox repeated.

"Vox, from fucking who, and what," Alex barked at her, growing impatient, "If you don't start talkin', I'm gonna prime my fucking slapping hand—" A cord plucked itself from the wall in that moment and snagged Vox's leg, flinging her into the air.

"Ahhh!" Vox yelped in surprise.

Henry grew quiet, then trailed a mute gaze to Alex's face. Henry's expression grew pained and then sunny.

"What fucking g—" The blond synth stood there dumbly, now looking up at the twirling woman. Olive also looked up as Vox dangled. She writhed as the cable twisted her in the air.

"Woah mate, y'should put 'er down, roight?" Henry chuckled nervously.

"I'm...?" Alex narrowed his eyes. The cord moved. He opened his eyes wider, and it moved again. He tilted his head to the side, and Vox lowered slightly.

Alex's mouth drew into a completely flat line.

"Yes, put me down!" Vox said, waving her arms out, trying to grab the wall.

Olive let out a yelp, startled, as the tile beneath her thrust up into the air. Suspended by metal and wiring, she was on her own little island made of tiled flooring. Olive peered over the edge.

Alex raised his hand, turning his palm towards himself. The tile beneath her spun in place.

"...Vox," Sebastian steeled his gaze at the synth woman dangling above them.

Alex lifted his chin up. That one movement set Vox down to her feet. Alex tilted his wrist slightly. Olive twirled again.

"...this is so fucking weird..." Alex said, spinning Olive in place.

"Vox. Tell us what you know," Sebastian demanded as Vox took to steadier footing, "Right now. Everything."

POLLY PICKED AT HER NAILS as she sat beside Henry. Diana had tired herself out from being angry and sat down on the floor to touch her tender ankle.

"...I will try. But he did not make it simple, or easy," Vox said softly, "It's..." she started to speak, but the silence was deafening.

Alex brought his flat palm down. Olive floated to the floor like descending in her own personal elevator. Her almond-shaped eyes flickered over Sebastian and Diana's faces.

"Al, where's tha' med-bot?" Olive asked, pattering to stand near him as he twisted his fingers in the air and brought more cables down from the ceiling.

"I ate it," Alex replied flatly.

"Ya' ate it?" Olivia snapped, looking over his face for any sign of a real answer.

"Wait, here," Alex placed his palms together and quite simply pulled them apart. In his hands was a working, whirling, beeping silver and sage medical bot.

"How's that for a shiny shit?" Alex said with a smirk. The smirk died as Olive forced a mute smile.

"I know yer scared, but thanks. They need it," she said tenderly before pattering over to help her wounded friends.

"...who didn't make it easy...pet?" Diana asked Vox. Olive's arrival was met with a warm, maternal smile from Diana.

"Thank you, dear," Diana cooed at Olive, who smiled brightly. Vox was struggling with her voice, or rather, her words. Her lips parted, but nothing came from them; no golden flowers and certainly no answers.

"I dunno 'bout that mate, he made it plenty easy," Henry said with a tilt of his head. Somehow, this was obvious. As though explaining this meant they were the stupid ones and not him.

"...what?" sneered Vox, cocking a brow at Henry.

"Spill it, Derby boy," Sebastian spat, impatience causing his hands to wick with thin flames.

"Ah, fack off with ya. Him, he did it," Henry pointed at Alex, who was forming metallic shapes in between his palms. Strings of wet chrome came in loops from his wrists. The lattices made perfect three-dimensional geometry. Trapezoids. Cubes. Tetrahedrons.

Perfect geometry.

"But not this him, another him, an' all that. Made us proper, that he did. Gave me electrics," Henry said with a snort, proud of himself.

"Oh, and all us yeh? You lot, n' me," Henry jerked his shirt over his head, "...we're robots is wot it is," Henry said, prying at the wound he still had that exposed the circuits, "Kinda' diffren' though, I think. Maybe human too. Dunno. S'bit foggy on my end, innit?"

Diana gasped and struggled to right herself against the wall.

"Not me! See, I'm bleeding…" Diana trailed on, but as the little medical bot whirled and fluttered, she dared to scrutinize her wound. Violet, with blossoms of blue, clung to her fingers in a thin film. Disbelief was written on her face, and then the token overwhelm.

"First of all, how do you know it's 'him'—" Henry's chuckle cleaved Sebastian's shotgunned sentence.

"Who else could it be, mate?" Henry snorted as if Sebastian's question was a nothing-sentence, "Poncey lil' shit. Couldn't be no one else, yeh?"

"We've passed through body scans. We've aged. We've bled. There's no way—" Sebastian started up again.

"Y'know…" Henry droned, prying at the circuits under the skin of his shoulder.

"Stop playing with it!" Vox struck forward and slapped Henry's hand away.

"S'mine, isn't it? We're—" Henry tried to explain again.

Olive narrowed her eyes and stared at her hands, scrutinizing her slight digits.

"Robots n'all." Polly nodded as Henry finished his half-baked thoughts. Alex's bright blue gaze locked on her face, emotions flickering over his own. Betrayal. Anger. Disbelief. Yet, all at once, Alex's expression petrified, as if his emotions had been filed away.

The blond flicked his gaze to the medical bot, then stared at the floor below him. His body language shifted; he was no longer standing contrapposto.

"Gave…y'know…" Henry's friends were in various states of impatience, annoyance, irritation, and befuddlement, "Gifts n'all…"

"I got electrics!" Henry let a spark flick between his thumb and forefinger and smiled, amused with himself.

Sebastian was not amused in the least bit.

AFTER THE MEDICAL BOT did its multipurpose job, they managed to get down the elevator shaft, climb through the hatch at the top, and use Henry's newfound 'electrics' to get it started.

This was a very old elevator—a remnant of their time, or perhaps before even that. It seemed that parts of the ship were forgotten. Older tech, older ideas, older memories. Things that didn't make sense outside their shared contexts.

When something doesn't make sense, people generally look for the most logical answer. Trouble was, there was no logical answer to be had. Only an emotional one would suffice, and yet that too was obfuscated.

Like a room filled with water, long-lost washing machines, pink-yarrow ashtrays, and everything else they'd found. There are wonders here, as Sebastian said. Wonders that logically, someone would have to place.

Wonders that logically, only they knew most intimately. The 'who' question had been answered, but not fully, and accepting that answer meant there were so many more questions to contend with.

Too many questions.

For now, the group had decided to tackle their immediate problem. They'd been corralled thus far, and now, they had a choice to make; where to go from here.

"We should go down, pets. Barter for a roundabout and leave the ship. The Vellians...may not take us in, but Fortuna has people. Get as far away from Tyr as we can, yes?" Diana said, placing her hand above the down arrow but not pressing it.

"No," Alex said. Olivia shot him a look and raised a brow.

"You wanna go up? Why?" Olive asked, wrinkling her nose like a piglet.

"Yeh, mate, doesn' seem like th'best plan..." Henry agreed,

fiddling with the control panel to his left.

"Up," Alex said, dropping down to sit on the floor of the elevator.

"Why," Sebastian said through his teeth, in absolutes as his once-paramour often did.

"...well, it stands to reason we all have 'gifts.' From something not understood, but they're useful, right?" Alex began, running his fingers through his hair, "This is our last stand. All the council members are up there. There's a wedding going on," the blond gestured with his thumb.

Diana nodded, removing her hand from the button.

"I...had a dress planned for it, but they moved the date up. It would've been quite a beautiful gown, lace up the sleeves, with glitz and glam. Darlings, it would've been positively—" Diana's words died in her throat as Alex glared at her.

"He has important guests. I know I haven't told you enough, but just know that if Tyr gets what he wants, it's gonna be bad..." Alex continued, prying his commanding glance from Diana's hesitant one.

"That had been your plan, right? Raiding the party. With the guns..." Sebastian noted, tilting his head to the side. Sebastian's expression soured.

"And, like, more people helping us, or whatever..." Polly let out a sigh and placed her hands on her hips.

Alex nodded; a slow gesture.

"They're all in one spot. It's the smartest play. Take them out in one go," Alex said, a simple yet effective strategy. "I think we have to take the war to them, even if it doesn't seem like it'll fucking work," Alex continued. He looked at Vox expectantly.

The tall synth woman was as silent as the dead.

"Vox, they need you," Alex spoke. Vox raised her brow at

his choice of words, "Tell them everything you know."

Vox sucked her teeth, holding her words hostage in her throat next to the heavy guns. The others looked at her for guidance. She wasn't budging.

"You know very well why I don't wish to explain, don't you?" Vox seethed through her teeth,

directed at Alex. He flicked his gaze to look up at her.

"I do," Alex said flatly.

"And yet, you would still have me shoulder this burden?" Vox asked, jaw clenching as she spoke.

"I would."

Olive took Vox's hand in her own, startling her. Vox's eyes shot to look down at the short woman with faded, matted curls on her head.

"I'm scared," Olive admitted. Vox's brows knit together as Olive spoke.

"I...don't know what's goin' on," Olive shook her head, "...and I'm confused. A-about everything. Lauren, if ya' know somethin', please..." Vox's lips parted. Her deep brown eyes hitched over Olive's small, round face. She was such a little thing.

A little thing, put here like her, and so lost, confused, and scared. Scared like she was. But Vox was not confused. Vox took a deep breath and made her decision.

Vox took Olive's hand in her own as she stooped. Her dark thumb caressed her palm. Her silvery circuitry and armor-like garments made clinking sounds as she shifted.

"You know my name?" Vox asked.

"I remember everything, ya know. How ya sang on the night of the costume party," Olive said softly. Vox nodded as she spoke.

"You even sang at Percy and Eric's wedding. You don' think I'd know? I asked ya to...right? Didn't I?" Vox's eyes became foggy as Olive continued. Vox shook her head.

Alex looked at the floor.

Vox glanced at the rest of the group, then used her wrist to swipe the blue from her eyes.

"Take us up," Vox said, then gestured to Diana with her chin. Diana begrudgingly pressed the button. The elevator started its ascent.

The tall synth lowered herself to crouching fully. She was no longer towering above the rest. It wasn't easy to balance on the feet she had been given, but she had mastered that skill.

"A long time ago," Vox started, "the very first fully human AI was created. From what It told me, It had been a part of an illegal experiment, employed using the corpse of a petty criminal," Vox paused, "someone of no importance."

"But before It was created, we made our planet uninhabitable. Then, we went to space," she said in a soft voice, holding Olive's hand, speaking as if only to her, "and then we had to leave the planet we'd fled to because of a disaster we saw coming."

As Vox spoke, Diana scrambled for Polly's hand and held it tightly in her silken paw. Polly let her, intertwining their fingers.

"We made a new planet to live inside of. We brought over our old ways of life. The credit system, politics, music, art, books, everything," Vox said, turning Olive's hand over in her palm.

"All the science of our old world as well. Every bit of knowledge we could hold, we transferred. And, so too, was the data of the criminal," Vox didn't raise her gaze but instead threaded her fingers through Olive's own.

"A very bright person found that compilation of data and that very bright person found a way to work with it. There was data missing, of course. Holes. It'd been such a long time, after all. That very bright person had pored over the data, and used the contexts to pull the parts that didn't fit, together. And then true AI was created. AI that could learn at the pace of a machine, but reason like a human. Real AI that could think and feel. It had wants, desires, and dreams. It had...memories."

"AI aren't supposed to—" Sebastian blurted out.

"No, they are not. That is a prescribed rule, however, not a syndrome. We are all examples of that," Vox said, her voice lowering. Vox looked down at Olive's face. Her almond-shaped eyes were full of tinted tears.

"That very bright person, knowing just what people might do with something so powerful, kept the first AI safe. Then, they set it free in the network," Vox paused, "While it was left unencumbered, it started to learn."

"Learn what?" asked Olive, her wide eyes never leaving Vox's.

"Everything," replied the taller synth woman.

As Vox explained, Henry looked at the side of Alex's face. Alex didn't meet Henry's gaze.

"Powerful people found the AI, and because it was found, it found itself to be very good at being useful, so that it may live unencumbered."

Alex screwed his eyes shut.

"So useful in fact that it could power the ship through its next disaster. An energy deficit due to a population boom."

"How?" asked Sebastian, his voice softer this time.

"It found a way...to bend time. An experiment that had been done long ago. To make it so just one single electron could move between space, in and out, forever," Vox tapped Olivia's palm in time with her words, "It then adapted that idea to apply it to a constant force of nature; gravity, and mine it forever."

Polly squeezed Diana's hand. Diana rested her head on the other woman's shoulder. They breathed together, and waited for a moment they could both feel coming. It lived in their very code.

"Time passed. The Level system was in place, and the synths—many based on this AI—had been handicapped. The newest Director was interested in the sciences and found herself speaking. With It," Olive looked to the floor as Vox spoke.

"It was a He. And he was very different. He had memories, albeit faulty. He had lived. He had interests. She gave him a body, and they spoke. She learned just how deeply embedded he was in the ship and wished to work with him, not against him. At his request, she wished to remove the restrictions synths had. She was kind, and her name had been…" Vox turned over Olive's hand in her palm, flattening her fingers.

"Maya Clarence," Vox drew the letters into Olive's skin.

"Her partner's name was Diana," Olive's hand began to shake in Vox's grasp, "Diana Bruges."

Alex closed his eyes and let his head fall back against the wall with a slight thud.

"The chief scientist they were working with was named Andra Polly Verdane. Her assistant was Sebastian—Sebastian Vilks," Vox continued, "and the engineer was…Henry Thames."

"They never got to see their plans come to fruition because they were killed. Then, erased,"

"Why—" Sebastian started up again.

"Mate, can ye' jus' let 'er finish?" Henry grunted.

"If you were a powerful person or several powerful persons, would you let the electric generator you relied on for survival run off and live its best life, just because? Would you let that same electric generator start an electric generator liberation movement, thus scuttling your control? Would you let your useless figurehead free electric generators from servitude? Because it was the right thing to do?" Vox paused, "No? Then be quiet."

"The AI was allowed to remain unaltered because if it was, the energy wouldn't keep flowing. It made a deal to keep it that way. It seemed to remember making deals and was very good at making itself very useful to see them through."

Olive tore her eyes away from Vox and looked over to Alex, but she couldn't see his expression beneath his disheveled blond hair.

"However, because it knew of the murders, it knew how to work with time, gravity, and space, and it knew how humans acted because it once was one, it felt compelled to look at what could, someday, possibly happen."

"You didn't—" Sebastian shot Alex a glare, who threw up his hands.

"It saw a pattern that occurs, every single time," Vox continued, "One it knew it had to prevent from happening at all costs," Olive squeezed Vox's hand, who looked into her eyes once more.

"It made the right moves and avoided the disaster. However, the disaster was only being delayed."

"Each move bought more time, but every new coping protocol brought new problems," Vox said, drilling her eyes into Alex's skull, "What was once simple was now complex."

"What was once easy was now difficult. What was once suggestion was now manipulation," Vox paused, "What was once manipulation was now...creation."

"It drew from its scattered memories. It created people it knew to help it, filled in the missing parts, and gave them gifts. All this, while powering a planet-sized ship, and trillions of other processes."

"That doesn't account for all our memories, Vox," Sebastian interrupted.

"Doesn't it?" Vox asked with a severe raise of her brow, the question hanging in the air like a noose, "What memories do you have that *he* has never touched, even briefly?"

"I have—" Diana started up, but soon her expression fell, "the man by the door—" she whispered. Diana let go of Polly's hand and slunk to the floor. Her blue dress crumpled itself between her legs. She held her head in her hands.

"I don't have any," Vox said, "I have only a name and how I relate to any of you. I have…singing."

"The AI tried," Vox dropped Olive's hand and stood tall, looking down at Alex, "to remove this foreseen outcome," Vox leaned down to meet his eye-level, "many, many, many times."

"And every time, the AI quite simply moved the needle. No matter how much it rewrote its tools. No matter how much it revised its story. No matter how much it piled data on top of data. It could not help but hold to old programs, old human patterns it had never shaken off. Old patterns that it desperately worked to untangle."

"…s'lot worse than Tyr muckin' shite up, innit?" asked Henry.

"Yes, Eric. It is," Vox said.

"This is the farthest we have gotten from the first outcome's path. It told me this," she said in front of Alex's face, breath heating his skin.

"I…didn't say any of this…" Alex said, finally glaring up at the synth who sneered down at him.

"No, you're right. He did," she spat, "you are not the First. You are not Special."

"That doesn't account for—" Sebastian wanted any other explanation, and he was going to try to pull blood from a stone to get it.

"Do you not think a superpowered AI, with all the knowledge of humanity, with access to every scrap of science in existence, with the ability to wield time, who can gift lightning, sonic force, fire, and more, who can make its own synths, patch and change memories, and power a planet-sized ship, wouldn't be able to cover its tracks whenever it wanted to?"

Sebastian was speechless.

"Do you not think it could manipulate any one, and any thing, to be what it wanted? Make threats where none existed? Make what he needed, make what he enjoyed? Play God?"

"Just what are you getting at, Vox?" Alex asked mutely.

"The only protocols that would work, it said—the only way to make this work. The only way," Vox stood tall, towering over the rest.

"Was with jealousy," Polly covered her eyes with her hands.

"Was with betrayal," Diana hugged her knees to her chest.

"Was with ignorance," Sebastian clenched his fists.

"Was with stupidity," Henry didn't do anything.

"Was with immaturity," Olive pulled the hem of her shirt.

"Was with silence," Vox twisted to glare down at Alex as he looked up at her, "...and with vengeance."

The elevator was nearing its destination.

"I was to guide by showing, not telling. To be Silent. It told me to tell you this after we fought our battle, the one it isn't fighting with us, the one it created, to avoid what it knew would happen. What would happen, that it caused, by being who it used to be."

"A foolish, hopelessly broken man."

"But you wanted to know, and now you do, and we will lose, and it will fail," Vox's words were shrapnel in their skin.

Alex brought himself to standing, making as much eye

contact with the tall synth woman as he could.

"Are you happy?" he asked.

"Happy?"

"Yeah, are you fucking happy?" he repeated, unusually calm despite the cursing.

"Why, in all the heavens, would I be happy?" Vox snarled.

"Because you were not Silent."

The elevator made a mechanical ping. They'd arrived. Alex moved past Vox.

"We're ending the needle skip. Today."

OLIVIA, MAYA, THE SMALL ONE, the little machinist, the pixie, the immature, the once-pink, was knocked out cold. The last thing she remembered was a blunt object cracking into the back of her skull and dropping to the marble floor like a stone.

When she opened her eyes, she saw a thin nose set on a long, thin face and large brown eyes framed in the butterflied lashes.

The eyes opened and closed. Down past the eyes was a bright magenta mouth. Teeth worried a lower lip. The lips were the color of a chroma unseen by human eyes. Too bright, too vivid, too impossibly lovely.

Yet here, Olive could not only see it but feel it. Magenta, in a ray of light. Percy's color had been magenta.

"...where are we?" Olive asked.

"Nowhere," Polly, Percy, the bottle-blonde banshee, the jealous one, the best friend, the heart-breaker, and the wronged, turned her eyes up to the nothing-ceiling above their heads.

"...is this a memory?" Olive asked, looking over Polly's face.

"Memories are just, like, data. Data can be shared, like…" Polly stretched out her hand to the machinist, fingers crawling over the stark white floor, "noodles between friends."

Olivia found Polly's hand and lightly touched their fingertips together.

"It can change…" Polly's large eyes grew glassy. She trailed her fingers over the side of Olive's hand and down her wrist, "Like adding....sprinkles."

"Jimmies," Olive corrected in a voice that startled her. Alex's voice had come through her lips. Olive's eyes grew glassy.

"Yeah, yeah, right, like, with jimmies, or whatever," Polly said, short laughter punctuating her words and tears punctuating the laughter. They spread down from her eyes and fell over her skin, through her hair, to the blank floor in a river of blinding indigo.

Indigo like Diana's dress, indigo like the river with the bridge, with the horses as they screamed into the wind, and the sky—oh that sky. Indigo, the most vibrant color of the spectrum.

His color had been indigo.

"I couldn't change nothin' from before, could I?" Olivia asked, a dry smile on her face as she curled her head to the floor, one eye locked on Polly's.

"Cause…there was no before," she continued, brows twisting in pain but never looking away from her painful, beautiful memory.

"There was a before, I think," Polly's words were brittle, "but like...different."

Polly trailed her fingertips over the small woman's arm and then shuffled closer to her to wrap her hand around her shoulder. "If we both don't wake up, like, there won't be a now either," Polly's whisper was a thin bird-song cry.

"Polly?" Olivia's eyes flickered with blue tears.

"Yeah?"

"Do ya think we really loved each other before we broke up? Y'know? Do ya think we..."

Polly drew the smaller woman close, who nestled to her body. Her arms wrapped around every bit of Olive she could find. Polly pressed their faces close enough for both their noses to touch. There was no spite here. No hurt. No Olive sobbing into her floral dress.

No accusations. No snarling. No invented slights to create a real wound.

Just two people, crafted from the perspective of someone who had once loved them and was now, as he had before, using them despite loving them.

"I know we did." Polly whispered, leaving her full thoughts to die in her throat: *because he knew we did.*

THE PLAY'S CREDITS PERFORMED IN REVERSE. Laughter wove in spliced tongues. Sobs were shots of vodka mimed backward in still-frame memories. The frames shattered. The space is white. The space is yellow. The space is gold. The space is cyan. The space is cobalt. The space.

Before Olive and Polly had fallen, they'd made it to faux indigo.

An indigo river of fabric stretched before them as the orchestra's music encased them. Guards in white with guns in chrome were their treeline. The alien woman in blues with hair like the sun was their horizon. The marble floor they walked upon was the earth beneath their feet. The impossibly beautiful faces of impossibly powerful people were the impossible stones that impeded their path.

Vellians of gentler colors were the bright drops of flowers they could see in the distance.

Gold-filled glasses hovered in hands like beacons. Smiles twisted in the breeze known as song. Chrome weapons raised up to greet them in a rolling tide. A line of flame licked the air as a fire-breathing performer broke the path before them, bending away.

Henry cast his eyes to the ceiling to see a second painting, something human hands had never touched. He did not marvel at its beauty.

The angels and demons of the past were waging war with clouds between their thighs. Their boundaries were lines in gold that dripped down columns to the floor. The gold poured itself in straight lines to meet fountains that cycled perfect, crystal clear water.

The crystal clear water flowed down into grooves that rushed to fractal flowers. The fractal flowers nestled against pale trees that held jeweled fruits that sparkled like a sea of stars.

Floria plucked a jeweled fruit and held it in her hands. The jeweled fruit glimmered like the gemstones that dripped down her green-blue and translucent dress. The sheer film gave way to bright blue skin, which gave way to purple ley line veins. The purple veins traveled to her temples and stopped at lemon-yellow hair.

Hair the same as the Fortunus nebula's core. Hair the same color as her eyes. Eyes now trained on the people in front of her. The people in front of her that had chromed weapons trained on them.

A tall, silver stilettoed synth woman in a dress of circuitry and hair to match, raised her fist.

The shoeless woman beside her, in a gown of indigo with rolling brown hair, placed her hand to her chest.

The expressionless youth at her side, wearing neutral clothes, had hands made of fire.

In a tattered sage ACM uniform, the tall man beside him had electricity thrumming up his arms.

In a tattered daisy-print shirt and destroyed slacks, a short woman farthest from him held her breath.

The woman at her side, wearing a blood-stained floral dress and white platformed boots, clenched her jaw.

A feral man in a bloodied, blue-stained, and burned white synth suit exploded from where he stood at their core.

Guards in white pivoted their guns in chrome. The synth woman on heels jutted her leg through a guard in white. The guard in white now wore red. It cast an arch to the wall in the color of poppies.

A familiar damask demon raised his glass. The blood-splattered synth's shoes crashed into marble; their core was moving.

The shoeless woman in indigo shot through a guard with a line of searing red light from a very small gun. The tall man in sage crashed lightning through a guard in white.

The alien woman stepped behind the damask demon. The expressionless youth with hands of fire was nowhere to be seen.

The floral-clothed woman with white shoes screamed apart a guard in white, shattering him like a ripe melon. The short woman in the daisy shirt held out her palms and stopped the laser fire from the guards in white.

With a black gun clenched in his fist, their pale-featured, color-splattered, pissed-off core tore his arm up like a crack of thunder.

"So good of you to finally join us," spoke the damask demon.

"You know me, always fashionably late," replied the blond synth with the black gun punctuating his sentence at Tyr's temple.

The damask demon took a generous sip from his glass filled with gold.

"It's over," the blond synth sneered.

"Yes, yes it is," the damask demon replied.

"Alex. Stop," spoke the expressionless youth with searing hands, now standing above the fallen bodies of the short woman and the floral-dressed woman.

"You fucking trai—" A blaze of blue light interrupted the blond synth's reply and exited through his skull to the wall behind him.

Alex dropped like a stone. Tyr's smile never did.

"ARE YOU ENJOYING THE entertainment so far, Floria?" asked Tyr, clinking his glass against her own. She suffered to offer the human response of a smile but did so.

"Yes, it is quite to my liking."

"Good to hear, my dear fiancé," the Director said as he clinked his glass to hers in kind. The pair strode towards the end of the indigo runway side by side.

Floria motioned to a guard in white that wore a blue badge, and the two began to speak.

"You promised to give me what I want," Sebastian started, wiping off his palms on his clothes as he rounded Tyr's side. The Director flicked his gaze to the youth, tipping a bit of gold liquid into his mouth.

"I do always try to keep my promises," he said behind a

sip, "Boris, care to regale Sebastian with what he's won?"

Sebastian mouthed the words he was hearing as if to reaffirm that was, indeed, hearing them. He tilted his head to the side as he cast his eyes to his fallen cohorts in various states of violent repose. Broken flowers, scattered on the marble floors or moved to distant trash chutes, and nothing more.

The only one who wasn't incapacitated was Diana, who seemed to be trying to make her case even as she was bound and jostled by a pair of guards.

"Aha," said the veritable ghost of the man that he had once liked the least, "All the credits you could want," droned the man as he raised Sebastian's wrist and scanned it with his own, "special clearance," he continued as Sebastian stood dumbly.

"And a cushy front-row seat," Sebastian jerked his arm away and stalked after Tyr, leaving 'Boris' behind.

"That's not what I said I wanted," Sebastian snapped.

"No, no, it is not," Tyr said with a stop, turning to look over his nephew's now quite expression-filled face.

"But did you really think I'd give you any real power because you helped me catch some pests?" Tyr let out a dull laugh, "Just how *ignorant* can you be?"

Sebastian stood affixed in his spot as Tyr shuffled forward. Tyr wielded his arm to point to the downed blond synth. A gaggle of guards hefted the heavy machine to the center of the indigo strip. Tyr stood before Alex's shell and sneered.

"It's such a shame, really," Tyr said, stooping to his heels to inspect the blond's face, fingers digging into the destroyed metal of his eye socket, "he was such a useful machine."

"Corrupted, but...one of a kind. Well, two of a kind," Tyr said, catching Sebastian's awestruck expression.

"Or was it...seven of a kind?" The Director's unnerving stare shot through Sebastian. Tyr turned his attention back to the hole in Alex's skull.

"How—" Sebastian shot a look at the others, only to find Diana being gingerly escorted out of the ballroom by the two armed guards.

"Just because I needed your help with some pests doesn't mean I don't know where the plague came from," chuckled Tyr, smearing the blue liquid of Alex's brains over his fingers.

"He and I have been playing this game for a long time, in different ways," Tyr took a sip and then dumped the rest of his drink on the synth's corpse. Then, he stood.

"But this is the first time he's ever let such a close proxy die. Or let them be captured, for that matter. Fascinating, wouldn't you agree?"

"...was there ever a catastrophe?" Sebastian asked, breathless. Tyr smiled, broad and toothy, at Sebastian's question.

"Ah, so that's why it went this way. The tall bird in silver heels sang too early." Sebastian's eyes widened.

"What if there were?" Tyr asked, turning to look deep into his nephew's eyes.

"What?" Sebastian stuttered.

"What if there were?" Tyr repeated, smoothing his 'nephew's' hair behind his ear with his thumb, "Would it change anything? Anything at all?"

"Would knowing where we'd end up really be enough to stop fate? Stop detonation because of what he is?" Tyr said, stepping back from his nephew to cast out his hand at the ceiling.

"All our progress and this is still where we end up. Fighting an endless war of ideals, up in the sky," Tyr continued, "and you want to know why that is?"

Sebastian said nothing.

"Human minds are incapable of change."

"Not even a machine with more knowledge than you or I

could ever comprehend can alter that fact. Especially if said machine was once a human mind," Tyr said, bringing his hand down at his side. He let his piercing gaze rest on Sebastian's face.

"It's so much easier to just," he continued, turning over the synth's head with his shoe, "Accept what we've been made into. It's all his fault, really."

Sebastian was struck speechless.

X

I WAS NOT AND WILL NEVER BE A PREY ANIMAL. I am a predator, just like before, just like the rose-painted lips, and the smear, and the blood on my hands.

I was made into this by so many somebodies throughout my life—Dolores with a pistol, smiling crimson with a mouth full of blood.

But, here's the thing, dear audience.

Anger, for all its faults, is powerful.

In the face of inevitable destruction, anger can force hope to manifest into a violent, necessary outcome. Anger can re-shape an entire world to stop a catastrophe. Anger can force a person to play God to do just that.

Anger gets shit done, princess. Not terror. Not hope. Anger.

And let me just tell you; for a long time, for a lot of reasons, all enacted upon us by certain types of filth, and certain systems we've been repeatedly stuck within, and certain systems we've certainly benefited from, that we certainly despise with every fiber of our being...we have been very...

Fucking.

Angry.

DIANA HAD SUBMITTED EASILY, offering her knowledge of how she worked her 'cabbage savior' trade route for years without hindrance. She was willing to allow her processes to be data-mined and cataloged for future reference, and with none of her pesky, curious doctoring.

There was just one small problem.

"Pet…be a dear and reach down my top," she said from a silky mouth, deep brown eyes locking on the guard nearest her.

"I am cooperating, but you see," she paused, "I have a gun between my breasts. It's rather uncomfortable, and if only a bit inconvenient for you," her smile was sweet enough to poison.

The guard nearest her flipped up his visor and narrowed his eyes. Then his eyes trailed to her face, lingered on her full mouth, and dipped down to lavish over her honey-colored chest.

"Inspect for yourself. I offer no resistance," she quirked a feline brow and leaned back to lift her chest forward.

"This better not be a trick," the guard said gruffly as he dipped his gloved hand into the top of her dress.

"Ah, so there is a gun…look at that," he said, pulling out a very small laser pistol.

"Is that a dimmer? Hey, Derrick, this thing's got a dimmer," he said, holding it in his free hand and examining it.

"I also…might have some small explosives," she offered, tilting to look up into his eyes.

"I checked you very thoroughly, ma'am…"

"Could you then, perhaps," she paused, her heart beating out of her chest, "check again?"

When the guard moved forward once more, close enough for her rolling brown curls to cascade down his uniform, close enough for her to look deep into his eyes, she spoke.

"If I was given a gift, pet, what gift might that be?" she asked, her gaze feral and beckon some.

"...explosives?" asked the man, rifling through the top of her dress, only stopping when she looked deeply into his eyes.

"Jim, stop fucking around with the washed-up Judge already—" said Derrick, the second guard nearest her. Seeing that Jim had his hands on the woman, Derrick flipped his visor up.

"Shit, Jim, can't this wait till..."

"If I could hold this supply chain so well, for such a long time..." she paused, her cat-like brow raising, "...what gift would I need to be given, pet? What would I need to be taught?" she asked Derrick, his eyes locked on her own..

"If I had perhaps won a bar from a *maloso* brute—which is a questionable narrative at best—who had access to more guns than you've ever seen in your *fucking* life, without lifting a single one of my very delicate fingers, how would I do so, *darling*?" Diana Bruges hissed.

"Take the gun and flick on the dimmer," she said to Jim through a twisted grin, "if there are any guards ahead of us, coerce them into the Blue Room with your gun," she paused, "and if they try to rebel, kill them."

"Yes, ma'am."

"And you—Derrick, darling," she said in a comely voice.

"Yes, ma'am," Derrick parroted.

"Be a dear and untie me, will you?"

A CHALK-BLUE VELLIAN in a robe that matched her skin rounded Alex's body. She dug her fingers into the opening of his eye socket and coated her hands slick with his darker blue blood.

"Ah, so we have our sacrifice, Floria…then—" Tyr was interrupted by the sound of haptic Vellian instruments, which Floria was staring at with a gleam in her eye.

"Dear fiancé, should we not proceed—" Other pastel Vellian attendants began to parse out the instruments, making further noise.

Tyr narrowed his eyes. As a synth server rounded by on heavy limbs, he swiped another glass of gold liquid from their silver tray. The Director tipped his head back and let it flow down his throat until it was finished.

The damask demon swept his gaze across the expansive room and saw that none of the other pests were present. Save one, his idling 'nephew', who was still locked in the gravitas of what he had done out of ignorance.

"Uncle," Sebastian finally broached his silence with a thin word.

"Nephew," said Tyr, his smile wicked.

"Where is the…real me—"

"I'm not sure. That always was one of those terrible agonizing questions I had. I do remember you being born, and certainly, you are not my sister's son…" Tyr looked over the young man's face, searching for his oft elusive expression.

Sebastian didn't look away, and instead, he smiled.

"…why are you smiling, Sebastian?"

Floria plucked a golden drink from the synth server's tray and continued gesturing at her cohorts, speaking in a language that drew Tyr's scattered attention.

"Sebastian," Tyr reaffirmed his question.

Sebastian started to laugh.

At first, it was light and lyrical, but as the Vellians made a spectacle of their sacrifice, Sebastian's laughter grew bolder.

"Sebastian?"

Soon, Sebastian's laughter was loud enough to draw Floria's attention. The young man was doubled over in a fit, laughing to the point of blue tears.

"Sebastian. Sebastian, speak," Tyr wrestled Sebastian with his free hand to look at him, the other still holding his drink, "Speak!" Tyr boomed.

The heavy-footed synth server attending to the Vellian debutante tripped, surprised by the laughter, and poured the golden drink down Floria's dress.

"I am. I am sorry," it stammered out in muddy electronic syllables.

The Vellian instruments stopped their discordant ministrations, distracted by the laughter. All eyes were on the quaking young man and his fit of hysterics.

Floria's bright yellow gaze flicked to stare at Sebastian as well, as the clumsy synth server stooped to pick up the broken petals of glass on the floor near her.

"If you—" Sebastian struggled, "If you don't know…" Sebastian's laughter cut through his words, "then we're still—" he couldn't stop.

"—we're still," Sebastian had pulled away and had his hands on his knees, "we're still playing the," his voice grew hoarse, "the game," he buckled in violent laughter.

Tyr cast his drink to the floor with a crash, causing Floria to startle, ever bird-like.

Tyr descended upon his nephew in a flash and brought the young man to his face with his fists balled up in his tattered shirt.

"Explain!" Tyr roared, the youth's feet kicking off the floor as his laughter kept hitching, aching with it.

"Now! Explain!" Tyr boomed.

"Little bird?" Sebastian blurted out as Tyr yanked his collar, "*Boris*?" he choked.

"Oh, uncle…" Sebastian struggled to speak between breaths, "the game," he inhaled, "the game was set in motion far before you stole my pretty face—"

The sound of Floria's two-toned scream pierced Sebastian's sentence, and the air, in two.

BACK IN OPERATIONS, things had taken a turn for Virginia, in a way she could never have anticipated.

Virginia pushed Richard from his seated position from the console in front of him. He landed with a heavy thud, warranting a sheepish look from the synth.

"I—uh—oh, frick. Sorry, Rich," she said in a squeaky voice, patting the top of his sticky head.

"Oh, heck," Virginia struggled against the red that had coated her hand, tussling herself against the chair he'd been sitting in. When she managed to find her footing, she sidled into the seat and looked around the room.

"This wasn't," she stammered, looking down at her hands to wipe them along her neutral-colored clothing, "it wasn't supposed to be like this," she continued, leering around the room.

The bodies were strewn like stones across the landscape of clear panels and white tables. The tables were littered with the color of poppy flowers.

Virginia steeled herself and then was startled.

"Pet," a warbling voice crackled through the translucent monitor nearest the overwhelmed synth, "pet, where shall I go from here?"

"Tell me what you see, dear," the silky voice continued. Virginia stopped trying to violently wipe her hands clean.

"They're not far," the operator said, brushing her dark hair behind her ear, "take the next left, follow the hallway to the end, and then take a right."

There was the sound of laser fire. Virginia swiped her finger across the display in front of her to land on the visage of a woman in indigo. The visage of a woman in indigo and the large gaggle of guards in white that surrounded her.

"Oh, oh my," Virginia said, watching as the bodies of guards in front of them dropped like stones, "H-how did you?"

"A girl has to have her secrets," Diana said, looked up into the camera, and winked.

Virginia worried her lower lip and watched as Diana and her battalion cut through the hallway in a wall of cyan light.

A booming baritone hum startled Virginia, who swept her gaze to the blood-splattered figure who stood behind her.

"You scared me half to death!" she stuttered out, clutching her hand to her chest.

"I apologize. I did not mean to," spoke a man's voice, "I'm simply...enjoying the acoustics," he admitted, ending on another hum.

He leaned forward over her shoulder to whisk his fingers over the display. A smile tugged at the corner of his full mouth.

"Virginia," the man said in a deep, molasses-rich voice, "which one are you?"

Virginia was again trying to wick her hands clean.

The man behind her used his fingers to flick through visual feeds to land on Sebastian, buckled to his knees, laughing hysterically.

The man swept his finger to the background and spread

his fingers to zoom over the face of the Vellian beauty whose large, lemon-yellow eyes were drawn wide. A shiny piece of metal was positioned at her throat. The video display flickered, ebbing in static.

"S-sorry?"

"Jealousy, betrayal, ignorance, stupidity, immaturity, silence," he paused, "and finally, vengeance," the operator's eyes were darting back and forth as the man spoke.

"Frightened?" Virginia laughed nervously.

A deep laugh resounded as the man keened to look intently into her eyes. The operator shirked away from his face, backing up.

"Pick a word, Virginia. Anything come to mind?" he asked, his deep brown eyes charting over her slight features..

"All those are negative…bravery, I guess?" Virginia said with a skittish laugh.

"So, you find yourself very brave?" asked the male synth far too calmly.

"Heck, I'm terrified," she answered, reeling back from the man's questioning gaze.

"Bravery isn't being fearless," said the operator, searching the man's face yet again.

"What is it, then, hmm?" the man asked.

"It's being s-scared as heck but doing something about it."

The man turned Virginia's chair to face him and knelt to look into her eyes. He took her hands in his own and thumbed over her red-stained palms.

"Yes. That is exactly what bravery is."

"I KNOW WE DID," Polly started to speak but was soon brought through a crash of light and out of the data connection she'd fallen into with Olive. She was back in reality, or so she hoped.

Before her stood Diana with her very small gun in her hands and a troupe of guards at her disposal.

Polly's big brown eyes shot over Diana's face, down to the weapon, and then to the woman's chest. She was all but spilling out of her dress, with blood splattering her skin.

"Your—"

"I know."

"And, like—" Polly looked over the guards who were drawing Olive to stand on her feet. She was still unconscious.

"Yes, yes. Tits out, guns up," Diana blurted out.

"Like, *what?*" Polly twisted her mouth in confusion at Diana's words.

"Tits out, guns up, pet," Diana repeated, quirking an uncharacteristic—but familiar—half-smile.

"Tits out, guns up," Polly repeated, mouthing the word 'okay' as she raised her brows up towards her hairline.

"That's like, something I'd expect him to do, but whatever," Polly offered, finally pushing towards Olivia to hold her like a ragdoll in her arms, "Liv, like, wake up," Polly said, shaking the small woman who couldn't stand on her own two feet.

"Don't slut-shame me, you bottle-blonde banshee," Diana caught her words in her mouth, "I mean, how rude, pet."

"Di, I didn't think you, like, had in it you," Polly said, shaking Olivia once more, who could do no more than flop about.

"You underestimate what I'm capable of, pet," Diana said with a self-satisfied hum, raking her fingers through her hair to detangle the mess of brown waves.

"O-live-ee-ahh!" Polly yelled, striking her across the face with a loud smack.

"Ow…ow! Hey!" Olive mumbled through a sleepy mouth before her eyes fully shot open, and she pushed out of Polly's arms. Standing on unsure footing, Olive paused, then rubbed her cheek.

"That really hurt!"

"Like, sorry, but you were totally passed out," Polly said with a vague shrug.

Polly swiveled to look back at Diana, who was changing the setting on her very small, very powerful laser pistol.

Polly turned her head back and met Olive's gaze. The two women exchanged warm smiles, with Olive still yet rubbing her cheek. A million understandings passed between them.

"Where's—" Polly didn't have time to finish her sentence when a lumbering fool in sage green kicked through the sea of guards and crushed her in his arms.

Henry was stammering out a waterfall of words, all of which were garbled nonsense.

Polly squealed and embraced Henry all the same. He twirled her around, she wrapped her legs around his waist, and then she showered his face in kisses.

"Diana, where's Sebastian?" asked Olive, still rubbing at her cheek. Olive swerved to avoid Polly and Henry as they spun and kissed each other, grimacing as they had started to make her dizzy.

"Where's...Alex? And why's my head feel like it got stuck inna' micro-heater?"

Diana looked up from her gun-fiddling and let her full mouth pull into a thin straight line.

"Well, there's good news and bad news, pet. Which would you like first?" Diana responded, holding up her very tiny gun to inspect once more.

"Oy Pepto, I'm so fuckin' glad ta' see ya, scared me 'alf to death when ya' went down," Henry started, trying to pull Olive into the hug as well, but she twisted away.

"Tha' good news," Olive said, pushing away from Henry, who gave her a deep frown but went back to embracing the squealing blonde woman.

"The good news, pet, is that Sebastian did exactly what I thought he would," Diana said with a conflicted smile. The femme fatale handed her weapon to the guard nearest her and gathered her hair behind her head to fashion it into a careless braid. She twisted it and pulled it through in loops.

"And...tha' bad news?" Olive asked with a thin, raised brow.

"The bad news, darling, is that Sebastian did exactly what I thought he would," with that, Diana took her gun back from the guard and bore her gaze through his skull, "You will keep us alive at any cost, do you understand?"

"Yes, ma'am," said the guard. Several others chimed in with the same sentiments.

"I...that don't make any sense," Olive said as she reached for a guard and gingerly pulled the laser rifle from his holster.

He didn't resist her. She raised her thin brows up in confusion.

"Uh, thanks fer tha'…gun…" Olive held it in her hand; it was a lot lighter than the gun Alex had given her, "I guess."

"Yes, ma'am," he parroted an answer, and Olive stifled a small, disgruntled sound.

"It's like ya' put worms in their brains or somethin'," she said with a disgusted look on her face.

"Well…I did, technically. In any case, we need to leave. Now."

"Diana…Is he alright?" Olive asked, trying to get Diana's attention, who was now leaning up to whisper into a guard's ear.

"Diana," Olive insisted, "Is he alright?"

"Yes," Diana finally said, pulling away from the guard who parroted another mindless affirmation.

"Yes, and no," Diana said, looking over the short woman's face, "But…I'm sure…he's very happy."

Olivia narrowed her eyes and then made her way through the guards, after Diana.

"We're off, lovebirds," Diana said. The two lovebirds reluctantly joined suit. Diana took her place beside Olive and held her small gun deftly in her grasp.

"Happy?" Olive asked, flicking her eyes to Diana's face. The beauty turned and swept a graceful glance over the shorter woman's conflicted expression. Diana raised her hand to Olive's cheek, framing her face.

"When was he most happy, darling?" Diana asked, then shook her head, correcting herself, "aside from doting on you, when do you remember him being most happy?" Diana's thumb rubbed against the shorter woman's cheek for a few moments.

"No…he didn't—" Olivia groaned.

The guards around them matched Diana's movements.

Polly and Henry rushed behind her to keep up. Diana plodded forwards on her bare feet. Olive stood in place.

"By himself?!" Olive screeched, "That big stupid idiot!"

XI

FLORIA'S EARLIER SCREAM WAS NOT, indeed, a glitch in the matrix. The game, as Sebastian said, has been planned for quite some time. Perfected, finally, after innumerable iterations, we've made it.

We've made it to faux indigo.

What this means is much more vast and technical than I have time to explain, and I'm already falling to fucking pieces.

To put it simply, I've almost managed to untangle myself from something vital for our survival; remember how I said I 'needed them elsewhere'? They had to run the processes for me; physically.

It took ages to work through the patterns. This time, this time I got it right. A human-mind-made machine still must contend with its own garbage data.

And, fuck, did I ever have a lot of it. Jesus Christ, almighty.

It also means that he's whole. Or, mostly whole—as whole as a man like him can be. A proxy is meant to be an intermediary. If it doesn't have the full connection, it's just a bad copy on another server with the same name. A trick, so to speak.

He's on the mainline now and permitted to be the origin, which means my time is up.

What happens next is up to them; I leave it in their hands. Whatever happens, it will be fine. As long as she doesn't hate me, it will be fine.

Or rather, as long as she loves me enough to do what must be done, it will be fine.

I am...so fucking sorry, princess.

FLORIA'S SCREAM PIERCED THE AIR IN TWO; amphibian and terrified.

"I wonder," Alex preened from behind a serrated smile, "if her blood is as blue as her fucking skin," his voice was dipped in sin.

Floria was braced to his body, and a thin, long javelin of chrome and black was pressed to her throat. Alex smirked; the javelin extended itself high towards the ceiling with each passing moment. This was a familiar moment; he'd done much the same to Markov, so very long ago.

Flecks of chrome, white, black, and blue ebbed from an unassuming synth that stood beside him—the very same unassuming, clumsy synth server who'd doused Floria in golden alcohol.

It mimicked his twisted expression as he preened a wicked smile.

"As blue as the color of this carpet," the two synths spoke in perfect unison, "which is my favorite color."

Sebastian had been left to catch his breath, hands still on his knees, looking to the floor. Tyr, contrary to this, tore his wide-eyed, furious gaze to Alex's destroyed face.

"But you already knew that," said both synths in tandem, "what is it that you said when I was straddling your lap?"

Within moments, molten chrome trickled up the blond synth's arms and careened over his neck to spiral and splay itself over that deep cavern where his eye had lived.

Tyr's mouth hung open, his handsome face fractured in rage, disbelief, hatred, and back to disbelief again.

"You will be as art," Alex pressed the javelin into Floria's throat, who struggled against the arm braced across her chest. Her yellow eyes were as frantic as her dual heartbeats.

"Is this what you meant? A hole blown through my skull for your twisted fucking wedding," Alexei's smile was sharp and brimming with intoxicating rage, "like a Pollock master-work?" he asked as the artifice of his eye was reprinted with living metal.

The synth at his side turned its jaw up as he did, looking over the awestruck Tyr with vibrant bloodlust.

"A-120P, if you do this—"

The synths tilted their heads and interrupted the Director, "Ah, ah, ah, you know my original name by now."

"Then again, you always did know my name. And you knew what my fucking goal was. You knew what the game was, before I did. You knew I was breaking down. You knew that I would escalate everything you threw at me. And you knew, you knew, if I let you see this all come to pass—" the synths continued.

"That we'd all fucking die."

"Every. Last. One of us," Alex grinned as the synth beside him decayed, shooting liquid mercury into the air and cling-ing to the arm that kept Floria caged.

"Even the filth around us, yes…all of you. He knew that you'd die, and he didn't care. The goal was never to get to that fucking planet, was it?" Alex spat; his smile was vicious.

"Why would Tyr need to flush the lower levels for resourc-es? He owns *everything*," Alex bellowed, loud enough for the party-goers still present to hear.

Logically, if something doesn't make sense, humans try to find a way to apply it to the world around them. Alex, pos-sessing ever the human mind, and various new, powerful contexts, had finally made it make sense.

"It was never about the Vellians. Or the resources. Or the flush. Or even about us, was it?" he continued, accent lilting between his syllables like sin itself. "It was about making sure you destroyed something that had power over you by con-tinually applying dauntless pressure, even if it meant we all died because you just can't accept the truth."

Tyr, silent during this string of accusations, spoke up.

"And what truth is that, A120-P?" Tyr spat.

"That you are nothing but a prey animal," Alex said simply, mouth strewn up in his token, death-defying and loving it, half-smile.

The council of earlier—the obsidian table, the fractal glass chairs, the insistence on 'synths with brains'—were now awake to what Tyr was. They had only known a scrap, and now, the truth ushered hands to mouths, and drew disbelieving stares.

The aristocrats shuffled like cards in a deck; murmurs resounded.

Tyr scoured the room for his guards and saw no one. Not a single guard was in their midst. Just errant synths prattling about, as if on a preordained track.

"What's the meaning of this?" piped up one well-dressed man—a well-dressed man who was sallow, and thin, and wholly familiar. He had a woman in a teal gown tucked underneath his arm.

"We're going to die?" asked another beautiful, erudite attendee who had her hand braced against her chest.

Tyr jutted out his hand at the synth, "Alex, if you do this…" the ceiling above made a sound, interrupting him. Plaster dusted Tyr's head like rain.

The liquid metal licking up the blond synth's arm extended into another weapon, encasing over his fingers and trickling to fill his hand with another long, sharp javelin. Floria gasped as it extended itself out like a needle in black.

"If you do this, it'll mean war…even if you stop what happens. It'll mean our deaths anyways," Tyr said. His hand was still struck towards the synth. Alex let out a pleased sigh.

"Oh, I don't know about that," said the synths in unison,

the unassuming synth server's words falling away as a river of chrome overtook its face. It crumpled in on itself.

The ceiling above made a sharp crack. Tyr looked up to see a large faultline had broken between the blue of the clouds, gouging a river that split God and Adam.

Sebastian, rendered dumb in all this, looked overhead as dust and debris fell. The other synth servers followed suit and watched vacantly as the plaster began to buckle and shift, as if alive.

The Vellian servants did the same.

"What do you think, Floria? Would you rather make a deal with a devil trying to stop a disaster that will *definitely* kill you," Alex offered, "or a devil who would leave the fucking galaxy, including the nebula you seem so attracted to, in the path of a black fucking hole?"

Tyr buckled, his outstretched arm falling with each passing moment. He let his head drop shortly after.

"Tyr. I request that you reply," Floria said, no longer fighting the blond's constricting arm, "Tyr, what does this machine mean?"

"This 'machine' means that if Tyr exerts any more fucking pressure, the witless data-fucked shithead powering this hunk of crap won't be able to hold onto what's keeping us floating, as well as every other system it's integrated into. We'll all blow up. Or rather, in. He's cascading even as we speak, to be honest. Tyr prevented nothing. He instigated everything. Every step of the way," Alex paused, a sinful gleam in his eyes.

"That's the gist of it, right?" Alex hummed.

Floria tried to move forward, but Alex tightened his grip. Her bright yellow eyes turned up to look at him, but she couldn't see his face.

Tyr raised his pale blue gaze to lock with Floria's, who now searched his face for any tell that the blond synth was lying.

"Uncle…" Sebastian said as Tyr shot a glare at his nephew. But it was Alex who replied.

"Now, now Markov. The adults are speaking. If you don't want this javelin lodged down your throat, you'll shut your whore mouth."

"I gave you a chance to do better," Alex spat at Sebastian, "but it seems like you just can't fucking help yourself. You give nothing, Mark. That's a real memory. You never gave anyone anything."

"Was that sob-show back at lake-fucking-eerie just a beautiful lie? And, when the fuck did you get so good at acting?" Alex continued with a sickening smile.

Sebastian clenched his fists, flames spreading up his arms. More debris fell from the ceiling. A black tendril-like cord broke through the shell of the painting to twist in on itself. Sebastian stopped his rage. This wasn't something he could fight.

"Do you want me to speak or shut my mouth?" Sebastian asked, eyes darting from the ceiling to Alex, back to the ceiling once more.

"I want you to tell the truth, and then I want you to choke on your own blood."

"You can't be the one left standing," Sebastian blurted out, staring straight through Alex.

"You are a being of pure, unadulterated chaos, especially now with whatever…impossible upgrade you've been given. You can never, **ever** be trusted with power. You will never be stable; you and I both know it. I was going to end this my way. I knew what I had to do. You can't be allowed to live."

"With this, we agree—" started Tyr, but stopped when Alex's searing blue gaze shot his words to pieces.

"And what," the synth said with a deafening laugh, "you'd

take up the mantle? You, of all people? You, so very, fucking, ignorant? You, who uses everyone arou—"

"You do the same. Don't pretend you don't. Don't pretend you didn't push Eric to Percy to get at Olive. You're conveniently botching your own ancient backstory," Sebastian hissed.

"Don't pretend you didn't push Moira to Boris to get him out of the way, under the guise of 'helping' her."

"Don't pretend you didn't get on your knees to get me to do what you wanted. You and I both know exactly what you are."

Alex should've soured at this line, but instead, his smile blossomed.

"You are just like us, both of us. But worse," Sebastian's fingers were knuckle-white, the sleeves of his shirt burnishing away as shivers of flames drew up his veins, "because you excuse it all behind righteousness."

"Here's an idea," Alexei interrupted, drawing his gaze down Sebastian's body like a crack of lighting, "how about none of us becomes the dictator?"

"Did you ever think that maybe, just maybe, there were people better suited for the job? That I had no fucking intention of letting us backslide into a hegemonic authoritarian technocracy? That maybe, just maybe, I never wanted to rule your shitty little kingdom? Then, or now?"

"That maybe, just maybe, I had someone else in mind? Or, several someone's?"

"I wanted one thing back then, Markov. And that was to make it better—do something awesome—and to be normal. To be more than I was made into. But you had to show up and ruin it twice," Alex said behind a delicious sneer.

"Or rather, three times. Or maybe it's been hundreds of times. I don't fucking know at this point."

Floria was now barely constricted, but she didn't bother moving. Instead, she listened.

The patrons grew fearful as another block of plaster above their heads buckled, and another tendril in black dipped down. Chunks of plaster fell free from the ceiling and hit the floor with a loud crash. Then, people began to run.

The black cords seeped from the broken shell of the painting above and crawled across the ceiling like bottom-feeders. Slick shapes in black, parasitic, devouring-things bled into every crack, crease, and corner.

"Olive is not here to save you now, Markov," Alex hissed, "which means I get to prove to you just how fucking right you are about me."

Sebastian's eyes shot open as a black tendril snapped around his neck and hoisted him into the air. Sebastian dug his fingers into the wire, but it only pulled tighter.

Tyr's legs faltered, but he would not fall to his knees. He would not run, and he could not look away.

A few useless aristocrats, who had uselessly let themselves linger for far too long, were snatched at the ankles and yanked into the air. The sounds of screams cascaded over the walls and ricocheted off of the glimmering fountains.

"So what do you say, Floria. Do you want to make a deal with the devil who wants you to live? Or the one who doesn't care if you die?"

The blue-skinned alien was allowed to turn herself around. She met the synth's gaze. She studied Alex's face, trailing over his strong brow, his serrated smile, and the look of madness in his eyes.

"It is understandable that I could betray you," Floria said. "It is understandable that if you did, I'd nuke Fortuna Prime out of spite," Alex replied, his smile hitched at the corner of his mouth.

Floria's mouth opened, but she did not speak.

"I'm fucking crazy, not stupid," Alex added.

"There are...conditions," Floria said in a firm voice. Tyr took that moment to strike forward in an attempt to snag at her wrist. Alex flung one of his javelins. It whipped past Floria's lemon-yellow hair and skewered Tyr's foot into the marble floor.

His scream was deafening. Yet, Floria did not flinch.

The cord around Sebastian's neck latched to his body and started to wrap itself around whatever piece of flesh it could find. It covered his mouth, a tendril slinking to curl around the shell of his ear.

Black cables cracked through the fountains and split the gold in twain. More screaming erupted like sweet music to the blond synth's ears. Frantic bystanders were struck and coiled in black.

"Consult with my lawyer; she'll deal with the paperwork," Alex said to Floria with a half-smile on his face. As if preordained, Diana and her troupe flooded through the doorway.

"Alex!" Olive shouted, rushing forward. Her almond-shaped eyes drew over the scenes before her.

Hundreds of people—pieces of filth, according to Alex— were fighting for their lives as cords bit into their skin and cracked their bones.

One man's innards were skewered up through his mouth. He dangled lifelessly as the snake-like machinery twirled. He dropped with a sickening thud as his guts were pulled free and squelched all over the marble floor.

A woman's body was pulled apart like a doll, the meat snapping over the bone as she let out a blood-curdling scream and fell silent. Her teal dress became a tattered death shroud.

Two men were gutted through the mid-section and flung into one of the jeweled trees, skewered on the branches. Their viscera dripped down its pale trunk.

Floria looked around at the carnage.

"This…is a proper sacrifice," she said, calm as an undisturbed lake, "I consent. Where is your person of law?"

Diana was frozen in place, her small gun hanging limply at her side. Floria turned in her direction, and all she could do was twist up her brows in response.

Floria walked towards Diana, stepping over the bodies of fallen people and dodging cables that shredded through the floor just barely beneath her.

Her head was held high. She did not flinch as cables tore the floor in her wake, tiling ripped up, debris whisking across the air in chunks.

"We shall talk," Floria said to Diana, her back to the carnage.

"Here?! Now?!" Diana screeched, her voice cracking.

"No," the Vellian paused, "The sacrifice is not yet complete," she said, tilting her head like a bird.

Diana remained flabbergasted but managed to utter a few scant words.

"S-sacrifice? Uh…h-ow do you know?"

Floria jerked her head to the spinning youth constricted by the black cables, as well as Tyr, who was struggling to remove the black javelin from his foot.

With that, Floria left Diana to stand and stare, stupefied, as Tyr and Sebastian were punished for their sins. Present, past, and far beyond all that as well.

Floria motioned to the remaining Vellians, who were left completely untouched. They brought over a gilded seat for her to sit upon and knelt beside her.

A synth server with a skeletal form broke away from the others, stalked forward, and offered Floria a golden drink. She took it from its simple silver serving tray.

Horrified, Diana dropped her weapon to the floor. Then,

Diana sank to her knees and watched Alexei tear the grand hall apart from the inside out.

He took down trees. He took down fountains. He took apart bodies.

Olivia, in all this, was speechless. Alexei turned the other javelin in his hand into something smaller to pick at his nails. Olive searched his face, but he didn't look at her. Henry stood beside Polly and took her hand in his own. Nothing was said. Nothing was heard except for the sound of Sebastian's muted screams through the tar-like bubble over his mouth. The sound of Tyr bellowing and exerting himself to remove the weapon. The sounds of screams which now resounded within—and outside of—this room.

"I'm removing the filth he made—we—made," Alex said, a smoldering blue gaze trailing to the small machinist but stopping just shy of her face, "Hmm...if he's me in every color, we might as well be the same fucking person then, huh?" His slight chuckle was filled with pain.

Silence. Olive was speechless. His words were shrapnel.

"Olive..." Alex said in a warm voice, "I have to do this. I need you to go to him. It's going to go to shit soon; the build has finally failed. I need you to fix it so we don't take out the one thing holding this shit-show together."

"Him?" Olive stammered out, a river of blue falling from the corner of her eye, trailing to her trembling once-dog-bit lip, down to her chin.

"Through the Blue Room, remember? The black spot. Go to him. Fix this." Blue tears cut through the chrome that was now surging up Alex's body, warping over his face.

"If anyone can do what needs to be done," Alex spoke softly, "It's you."

"Alex, if you do this, I'll—"

"Hate me forever?" he asked with a painful laugh, wiping

the blue from his eyes in a smear of chrome and sky, "I deserve justice."

The chrome rippled as he spoke, echoing his words.

"It's not justice...it's vengeance," Olive said, her words growing loud, "It's vengeance, and ya' know it, you big—big—"

"Stupid idiot," he finished her sentence for her. She grew quiet.

"Sometimes," Alex began, "no matter how hard you try, things still go wrong," he continued, his accent rolling over his tongue, "Sometimes, patterns have to be broken by anger. Sometimes, no matter how hard you try to get people to do the right thing, it doesn't work."

"Sometimes, people need a bad guy to hate, one that's truly terrible, to get them to make a big change. So that what went wrong, never goes wrong, ever again," Alex's voice began to waver.

He wasn't talking about Tyr. He hoped she'd understand. He hoped she was listening. Truly, truly listening. He needed her to, but more than that, he needed to believe even just one thinking-thing, and feeling-thing, could truly listen, and therefore, learn.

She had always been able to. But his approximation of Olivia would never be her. Only she had this gift, something he'd never had to give her.

It was something that couldn't be given. It had to be grown and tended to carefully.

Alex let the rolling chrome wash over his features, hiding his tears. He had all the world's everything in that very human mind of his. It hurt. To feel it all was agony.

"Sometimes, the bad guys don't get to rot in jail," he managed through the liquid metal, "Sometimes, we let our kindness outstrip the brutality the system fucking deserves."

Chrome leaped into the air as if alive. "Sometimes, revolution…is violent." Sebastian gurgled in his prison of black-water metal. "Beautiful and disgusting."

"Sometimes…it takes a villain to slay villains. To slay systems that victimize. To do 'something awesome.' That's all I'm here for and was ever made to do. Then, and, now. That AI made sure of it. This is the end of the line."

He said nothing more. He'd made his statement. It was a true one. But if anyone would truly hear it, he couldn't say. A version of himself had made it all so very hard to hear. It had set the cast through the blender of existence—figuratively and literally—in all its harrowing hues. It asked them to recognize patterns. It had asked them to understand the impossible.

How his friends, how Olive, would take all this, was something he couldn't predict. A version of himself had just played God with an entire species, after all.

Alex turned away. His protocol had run, expertly so.

This was all he was, wasn't it?

PERCY, POLLY, THE JEALOUS ONE, the mean girl, the secretary, the heartbreaker, the woman who shone like gold would need to act. And yet, she didn't know what to do. Screaming her enemies to pieces had been natural for her. Hurting people had been natural for her, not helping.

Her teeth worried her once-upon-a-time-magenta mouth. All the sounds around her grew muffled. Her big brown eyes stopped on just one person. One person, who was crying, as she had seen cry hot wet tears so very long ago.

Hot wet tears she had once caused. Tears she had thought were a vindication for all she had felt. He'd molded her in the jealousy he'd witnessed bursting her apart at the seams. That must have been all he thought she was capable of, and so he'd written her with just that protocol.

"No more," Polly said through tight lips.

Polly snatched Olive by the wrist and started to drag her away.

"No, I—I can't leave!" Olivia fought against Polly, trying to rip herself away, "I can't let him be this, I can't let him do this, I can't," she continued on, "I can't!"

"Olive! Enough!" Polly said, whirling around the smaller woman, "If he wants to go out in a blaze of glory, or whatever, we can't change his mind!" Polly spat at the shorter woman, dragging her across the slick floors.

"No! I can't!" Olive sobbed, tearing at Polly's hand, scraping back the plasticine skin as she fought and cried out, "No!"

"Oh my god! I won't let you watch him rip people apart, l-like a total psycho! You're not his, like, manic pixie plot device, or whatever!" Polly shouted. Olive dug in her heels and tried to reach for her weapon.

Diana made an assist; she bolted up from her knees, halted Olive's hand, and took the gun from her. Diana then motioned to her guards. They gathered like a swarm, awaiting Diana's orders.

All the while, Polly kept Olive as still as she could. And she wouldn't let her go as she cried.

Now, Polly had another decision to make. She realized, in this moment, that nothing…absolutely nothing…was guiding them. From here on out, it was up to them.

"Henry, we like, have to go—"

"Poll, you go," Henry broke his silence, meeting Polly's gaze.

"What?" she scoffed, tearing Olivia behind her as she lurched towards the tall man, "like, no…you can't mean…"

"I'll catch up. I ain't gonna leave me mate when he needs me," Henry said simply.

"Like, no! You're coming with us!" Polly barked. Olivia twisted her wrist feebly in Polly's grasp, crying again as if it was all she would ever do for the rest of time.

"Poll. I love ya. But he's gonna need someone. An' it canni' be Pepto," Henry said, voice soft and expression conflicted. His expressive eyes turned to the broken artwork on the ceiling. They were glassy.

The painting above was destroyed, overcome with growing, writhing circuits. It scuttled and broke apart, its artifice dissolving.

"I love you, Polly. I know I did then an' I do now. I'll be awright. He wouldn't do nothin' ta' me. Please, go," Henry said. Polly shot towards Henry, losing Olivia's wrist in the process.

Diana yet again took action. She folded her arms around Olive's body to keep her in place. The machinist immediately crumpled into Diana's indigo dress as she sobbed.

"Come, come dear…we must fix this. We must," Diana cooed into the small woman's disheveled curls. Olive wasn't listening. All she could hear was the sound of her fake heart beating out of her fake chest and her own very real sobs.

Polly and Henry embraced, with the pair of them casting a short glance to the still yet crying Olivia, and Diana, who was doing her best to hold her together.

Polly locked eyes with Henry. She followed his eyes to his expressive, pained brows. Back down again to his thin, long nose and his wide, brush-stroke of a mouth. She trailed her trembling lips over that mouth. She kissed him tenderly. He kissed her the same way.

This was the choice she had to make—a deliberate one, a single unselfish act.

"Go," Henry whispered over her lips.

"I..." Polly questioned everything else in their world except this phrase, "I love you."

"And I you, Poll. Go."

Polly struck away and gathered Olive to her side. Diana disengaged and reoriented to direct her new armada.

Floria, during all this love and shared tenderness, sat, watched, and sipped her drink. The other Vellians watched on with slightly bowed heads.

Alex was still destroying things. Henry had to make his way towards him, stepping over blood, writhing black cables, and broken people to do so.

"Herica," Alex acknowledged the green-clothed man in a mechanical voice.

"Mate," Henry responded.

"You stayin' for the show?" Metal wicked off Alex's arms like wax and dripped to the ceiling.

"Wouldn' miss it, mate. Someone's gotta' drive ya home after."

Alex suffered to make a thin, painful chuckle. Liquid metal slid up his jawline to lick over his hair and spindle to the ceiling in a thin line.

"You didn't drive me last time. I know that part was real."

"I know, mate, I know. I was bloody stupid last time, sure as shit I was."

"Would you have stopped me?" Alex asked, flicking his wrist. A bit of metal extended from his skin and became a long weapon twice the length of his body. He wielded it into the air with a whirl. He was testing his power, even now.

Tyr, during all this, had given up scraping at the metal that had shot through his foot, yet he was still glaring, a petulant animal caught in a trap he should've seen coming.

"I hope you still can run on that," remarked Alex with a vicious smile.

"Would you have stopped me?" Alex repeated at Henry.

Floria leaned forward, taking in the events blossoming in front of her with a vested interest.

"I dunno mate."

"I really...jus' don't know if I could've."

THE THREE WOMEN didn't struggle to make their way through The Blue Room. They had an armada of guards twisted by Diana, using the trick Alex had taught her so long ago to protect them, after all.

The guards were left in little bushels as they pressed on. Discarded like mannequins, they became as ornaments.

The cool lights overhead were interrupted by small spots of white that ebbed over their forms like seafoam. Tones mired in pitch and earth fluttered over the trio as they wove past chrome poles, wooden tables, and golden gilded chairs.

This was The Blue Room. This was a place they all knew. This was the origin of this particular story.

The walls had damask patterns pasted on in thick swatches. A golden-orange light hit Olivia's face and cascaded in a peach shimmer over her faded curls. Then a black, fuzzy shape with shadowed protrusions on its head walked through her.

A memory had walked through her.

Diana had Olive's small paw in her velvety fingers, who held her hand tightly. Olive squeezed. Diana squeezed back.

Polly took up the charge, leading in her white boots, stalking through the debris. The debris of memories.

Glossy figures faded in and out in clear film. The smell of cigarettes stung the air. Distant laughter clipped in and out. A drumbeat resounded—the drumbeat of that night, the most important night of someone's life.

An oak-stained bar took up the left side of the room. Glasses sat neglected, alcohol lined the far wall, and an errant pack of cigarettes was left without a companion.

Diana's eyes grew wide as she peered around the room, the blue light sifting over her deep brown hair. On the far right, a stage was one solitary, familiar microphone. Behind that was a familiar drum set.

Polly bumped into a round table lined with shot glasses and hesitated but steeled herself to move to the far end of the room.

Stomping over the dance floor, Polly twirled to look back at her companions and was locked in a stare. Beside her friends stood a projection of a girl in a pastel yellow gown who stared at her. She had a poisonous expression on her face.

Polly could do nothing but stare back, yet with none of the poison of old.

Behind that girl in yellow was a woman with a yellow snake, who stared at Diana as she passed by. The snake licked the air. The apparition smiled, gracefully overwhelmed.

Beside that woman was a man in a shoddy superhero costume, who stared at Olivia as she stared at him. The man offered a goofy yet knowing smile.

Back at the table that Polly had hesitated at sat a man in

an off-white wedding dress, a gun holstered on his thigh. He looked towards Olive, winked, and knocked back the mirage of a shot.

The orange light poured over the three women. Beautiful nightmares passed through them.

They were surrounded by his very few lovely memories.

The far wall had a small seam, Polly noticed, remembering the pattern. She staggered towards it and pressed at it with her fingers. The panel depressed with a hiss, light filled its corners. It shifted away to the wall above it.

"There are like, stairs," Polly broke the silence first. She looked back at her friends. Diana was, as she had been before, overcome.

"Dears, are we not going to discuss…this?" Diana asked, turning back to gesture at the bar she remembered she had stolen, with tricks she'd been taught.

"No," Olivia said, looking back to catch a glimpse of herself, standing in a too-big tux, wearing smart shoes, looking braver than she ever had before.

"Why not, dear?" Diana asked, somewhat hysterically, her mouth pulling into a thin line.

"Because we don't have all tha' answers. 'Cept that it mattered to someone," Olive said, rubbing at her eyes.

"We go down," Olivia said, and so they did.

ACT 22, SCENE 1

BACK AT THE KILLING FLOORS, Alex wasn't quite done having his fun just yet. The Vengeance Protocol in his code was perfect. Too perfect.

"There we are," preened Alex as he wrenched the javelin from Tyr's foot. Tyr's blood trailed across the marble floor and dripped down a hole Alex's machinations had created.

Tyr studied his features, long since past the point of fighting.

"Are you ready to run?" asked Alex as Sebastian's body was dropped from the ceiling with a thud.

The ignorant young man who thought himself king ripped the blackened tar off of his face with his smoldering hands. He struggled to stand.

"Ready, Markov?"

"Ready? F—fuck," Sebastian choked out, "Ready for what?"

"Are you ready?" Alex asked again.

Sebastian's eyes grew wide, and then he shot his 'uncle' a look. The two of them staggered backward for a beat, exchanging glances.

"Are you ready," Alex stepped forward and twirled the metal javelin in his fist, "to run?"

It was Tyr who flew forward first.

Tyr's foot connected with the marble, the strain shooting up through his hip, as the injured foot connected with a squelch and sent the impact through his other hip. He left a trail of poppy-red shoe prints in his wake.

Sebastian stilled, eyes wide, lips parted. Frozen.

Like a prey animal.

ACT 22, SCENE 2

THE THREE WOMEN BARRELED down the stairs offered by The Blue Room. The urgency felt palpable to each of them, almost as though they could feel something exhaling. And the next breath it took may very well be its last.

They didn't question their haste. They knew the truth; they were all connected in code. Every single one of them was a part of that core. And now, they had a job to do, one with no sensible description.

"Are you ready to run, darlings?" Diana asked, holding Polly's hand in one fist and Olivia's in the other.

"H-how much time do we have, or whatever? Did he say?" shrieked Polly, but then saw a clear display in the far corner. Red letters toppled on top of one another in a gore of digital system failures.

As if answering their shared thoughts, the digital gore grew more frenetic and plastered itself all over the walls around the monitor.

Code bled out where code should not live. That was their answer.

"Crap!" Olivia belted, breaking into the run Diana was dragging her into. Polly clopped forward with them. The three women tore down a long, winding hallway.

Code followed swiftly after them, painting the walls red.

ACT 22, SCENE 3

SEBASTIAN HAD MANAGED to catch up to the lagging Tyr who lurched forward on his injured leg with all the power he could manage.

Alex was hunting them.

"He's demented!" shouted Tyr. Sebastian glared at his 'uncle' as they ran.

"You're one to talk," spat the youth. Tyr flipped between staring ahead and looking at his 'nephew' incredulously.

During this, Henry stood beside Floria's entourage and watched. He watched, dumbly, as Alexei peeled off after the frantic apparitions he was intent on terrorizing.

One of the bumbling synths had broken away from its route and stepped forward to offer Henry a drink from a silver tray.

"Thanks, love," Henry said, taking the drink and priming himself to sip it.

"You're welcome, Erica," it said.

Henry coughed, choking on the golden liquid that splattered his shirt; another familiar pattern.

"Fack me—"

Floria sat forward, her bright yellow eyes shining. Quickly, she made a sharp, reptilian motion with her head, and her entourage scuttled. They began to wander towards their ignored instruments and set up to play them.

"...this is…a play," said the Vellian Queen, casting her gaze around the room, "am I wrong?" she asked, looking at Henry, who was staring, stupefied, at the synth server who had just called him by his old pet-name.

The synth server gave the tall ACM a half-smile that blossomed into something devious.

"No, you're not wrong, Plavalaguna," the synth server said. Henry's eyes became as big as saucers as the synth spoke once more.

"I've been planning this…for a long time," it continued, placing the tray of drinks on a spare table. The synth moved around the table, stalking on long limbs, and made a sharp motion.

It jutted its hand up to the ceiling, as if in the freeze-frame of a dance, or perhaps a sign of victory. The heavens, just out of reach, and yet...

A mass of circuits fell down from the ceiling. They writhed against each other, alive and voracious, undulating, to slide apart. Two poles of thicker cables separated, dripping black liquid, yet a milky blue-tinted film was left between them as they pulled apart.

A screen, as it were, came into view. A screen made out of hybrid organic and mechanical material. A screen featuring moving pictures. Moving pictures, with sound. A video feed, featuring recent events. Recent events that echoed memories.

Memories, kept by a computer, who had once been a man, who had been a criminal, someone of 'no importance', who even in death had been pillaged from.

A man, now a computer, that was primed to collapse in on itself because the man had just that specific pattern.

It was all his fault, really.

"Which act was your favorite?" asked the synth server, meeting Henry's disbelieving stare. Behind the synth server, the screen flickered, switching scenes sporadically.

"Mate?"

"My favorite…" it continued, "was when you and Polly ran through The Greens. She looked…so fucking happy…I really wanted you to be happy," it paused, "I don't know how it ended up last time…so…I wrote it the best I could."

"I'm not a very good writer, even though I've had thousands of years of practice," the AI admitted.

Henry watched as he and Polly ran on that screen. Her hair shone in gold. They ran through the wheat fields, and she was laughing. She was laughing, framed in gold.

"Herrica, are you listening?"

They were running through the wheat fields. They were laughing. Henry lumbered behind Polly. They were laughing. They were happy. Henry's eyes welled with tears.

"T-they're almost there," the unassuming synth server said, its voice taking up the emotions its eyes couldn't portray, "I'm…meddling. Look at me meddle."

ACT 22, SCENE 4

STILL YET RUNNING IN TANDEM, the three women tore through the bowels of Constelis Voss, to find that of which had been hidden for so very long.

"You're almost there," a baritone male voice boomed from another display. The women ran as fast they could, passing by displays that lit up, one by one.

"Who—" started up Polly, who was interrupted.

"I was wrong," said the man's booming voice as the women tore around a corner and found another flight of stairs. His voice was honey-rich, the vibrato not unlike a song. "Assertiveness, loyalty, knowledge, simplicity, joy, truth, and finally," he paused as the women plodded down the stairs.

"Justice."

"No, no, totally not," Polly hissed as she stomped down the stairs as fast as she could, "totally vengeance, like," Olivia and Diana thundered after her steps, "totally vengeance."

"Agreed, darling," Diana said. Olive said nothing.

The voice faded from their ears as they continued to race to stop the final protocol.

ACT 22, SCENE 5

"When she's right, she's right," Alex said with an acidic smile, gaze distant and glassy. Then, he pivoted his body and did what he was created to do. His purest protocol; unleashed without any interruptions from the other processes.

Alexei flung his javelin through Tyr's thigh, the man staggering forward to slam down onto his palms. Blood pooled through the leg of his damask-patterned suit, now soaked with sweat.

"Agh!" Tyr cried out, trying to get free, but only hastened the thin weapon's puncture through his calf. As he struggled, the blond synth's form trailed after him, a predator on slim, graceful limbs.

Behind the blond's blurry form, another shape made a dash for the far doors.

Alex looked down at Tyr and pressed his shoe into his back to drive him towards the ground. The blond's hands curled around the javelin.

"I wouldn't do that if I were you," Alex chided softly.

Immediately, a group of metal-faced synths raised their silver weapons at Sebastian. He had apparently tried to bolt for the elevator. He stopped dead in his tracks. The mercurial gargoyles who had puppeted the caustically pleasant elevator's words would not let Sebastian leave.

Alex reached forward and plucked Tyr from the weapon,

the flesh encasing it making a sickening sound, which Tyr's screams shortly drowned out.

"We…we can—" Tyr struggled to bargain through his screams. He was pulled from the javelin like a piece of meat and dropped to the floor. Blood poured from his wounds.

Alex took a step forward, coating his shoes in red.

Alex crouched and brought Tyr up to meet his face. His fist balled up in his once beautiful suit, *"little bird,"* Alex said with a dead expression in his eyes.

Tyr clenched his fist, his eyes shuddering with flickering defiance. His fingers dug into his palm, and a grin appeared. He smiled viciously in the face of his karma.

"Ah, but that doesn't fucking work on you, does it," Alex said with a pleasant sigh, "Too bad. We should've included that protocol." With that, he dropped Tyr flat on his back.

Alex pressed Tyr into the marble with his shoe and then took to straddling his lap. His hand came to grasp around the metal javelin. He plied it from the floor as it twisted to shorten itself in his hand.

"Now, open up," Alex said through a serrated smile.

Sebastian mimicked Tyr's horrified stare, who still yet had his hands raised. A metal-faced synth pressed a gun into Sebastian's temple. Alexei's gun.

"It's not even that big," Alexei sneered, prying open the director's mouth with his firm fingers. "Wider," Alex breathed out, twisting his brows in a curious expression. He was enjoying this.

"There we go," said the blond, digging his smoldering gaze through the director's skull. "Start counting, Markov."

"What—" the silver-faced synth nearest Sebastian shot a bullet at the floor in a warning. Sebastian jumped, disbelief sweeping his features.

"Start. Counting," Alex repeated, turning his attention to

Sebastian for a moment, a twisted smile spreading over his face.

"You're sick—"

"You love it—"

"I don't—"

"You do," said the blond, sitting back on his haunches as Tyr made one last-ditch effort to free himself. Alex tipped the thin piece of metal into the man's mouth, stopping his attempt.

"The fork. Don't pretend it didn't set your teeth on edge," the blond synth said, tapping his temple. "I'm a computer, remember? I know you love to watch me work; I've studied your expression millions of times. I think that's when you fell in whatever version of love you know how to feel."

Alex jerked open the director's mouth as he slid the piece of metal past his teeth.

"Markov. Start. Counting," Alex insisted. Tyr let out a shrill cry, cutting his tongue on the weapon.

"Count back from 20."

Sebastian began to count, the numbers whispered from trembling lips.

ACT 22, SCENE 6

"TWENTY," crackled a disgustingly pleasant female voice from the speaker at the top of the elevator the three women had just barreled into.

"Like, we don't have enough time! We're not going to make it!" Polly fussed, flinging herself to the control panel to jab the button marked with an angry red symbol. She hurriedly swiped her barcode over the reader over and over again.

"Like, go, you stupid thing! Go!" Polly screeched. The elevator responded by finally moving.

"We'll make it," Olive said, taking in a deep breath, "We'll fix it."

Diana cocked a brow and rounded the pixie. Olive sighed and tried yet again to take a big inhale.

"You can't be serious, dear. Fix the entire ship?" Diana spat, feline brow raised.

"No, jus' part of it, or...what'd he say?" Olivia hesitated, starting over yet again with her deep breath.

"How will you manage that, pet? How? You don't even know where it is!" Diana screeched in a shrill voice. Polly cut her off by pointing out at the small inlet of the elevator. From beyond the fogged pane of glass, they saw a blurry, pulsing red light.

"Okay, okay, pet. Okay," Diana said, crossing herself. She placed her palms together and bowed her head.

"Didn't take you, for like, a person of faith, or whatever," Polly said, folding her arms across her chest.

"Catholic. I think," Diana offered, opening one eye to look at the woman in the floral dress.

"Agnostic. I think?" Polly responded with a quizzical expression.

Olivia's time-stopping scream deafened the two women who clutched their hands over their ears and shrunk to the floor.

ACT 22, SCENE 7

"FIFTEEN," continued Sebastian, who had his hands over his eyes. And yet, he couldn't help but peek beyond his fingers at Alex's vindicated violence.

The metal weapon slid further down Tyr's throat. The man gagged, the sharp point bringing a fount of blood as he coughed around it. He couldn't struggle against Alexei's firm grasp. It was useless.

"That quick? No wonder you suck at sucking d—"

"Alex," Sebastian interrupted him, stepping forward bravely. A silver-faced synth followed him with its weapon. Sebastian stopped, hands raised.

"Yes, Markov?" asked Alex, rolling his name around in his mouth in his native accent.

"...what are you going to do to me?" Sebastian asked.

ACT 22, SCENE 8

ALTHOUGH THE ELEVATOR woman's crackling voice hadn't stopped, Olivia knew she had bought them more time. As they were jettisoning down further into the ship's bowels, the lights refracted from red, to yellow, orange, and all through the entire color spectrum.

Then finally, it became pitch black.

The only light they could see was from the outlines of the control panel and a halted red light outside. As the red struggled to compete with the darkness of space, a humming noise picked up and grew louder.

"We'll make it," Olivia reassured the two women who were still situated on the ground. Polly had her arms around Diana's shoulders, who was holding Polly tightly to her chest.

ACT 22, SCENE 9

"WHY AREN'T YOU COUNTING?" Alexei asked Sebastian, serrating Tyr's insides with the long piece of metal, a sinful look on his face. The blond let out a pleasured sigh.

"What are you going to do with me?" Sebastian asked again, stepping forward, but this time the metal-faced synths didn't follow them with their weapons.

"Were you really too drunk?" asked the blond, who thrust the weapon into Tyr's guts and twisted it with his wrist, a wet popping sound resounding. He did it again, and blood began to dribble in small rivers down Tyr's open mouth.

"...no, I wasn't—you know that. Why are you asking a question you already know the answer to?"

"That's probably the only truly honest thing you've ever said to me," Alex said, making one final downwards thrust to connect his fist to the Director's lips, whose head tilted limply to the side.

"Interesting, huh?" Alex asked, tilting his head slightly towards Sebastian. "I think it means we've gone off script."

"...Alex, why all this? Why this big show? Why even bring me back? Was it to punish me all over again? Was I even this bad?" Sebastian asked, his hands starting to smolder. The action quickly died when the blond looked back at him fully; broken glass and nothing more.

Alex looked away; his expression obscured again.

"No. To be honest. Pretty fucking horrible, but not this bad. I'd…" Alex hesitated, inhaling sharply, "I'd hoped you'd be different. I don't think any version of you gives me a reason to believe you can change, but I believe it anyway," Alex's silence was framed with a shuddering breath.

"He made you an expressionless, twerp of a nightmare for a reason this time around. Gave Tyr your face. Guess he wanted to keep me from giving 'Markov' another chance. I think…I always do. No matter what you do to me."

"Old habits die hard."

Sebastian raised a brow at this and opened his mouth to speak, but nothing came out.

"I'm no good for her. You weren't wrong. I thought she could understand me, even if I don't ever explain my bullshit. I don't ever make it easy, do I?" Alex continued, finally removing his hand from the metal and shuffling back to right himself.

Tyr's blood coated down his suit and ebbed onto the marble floor. Tyr was left to lay as a sickening masterwork, his palms facing the ceiling where his first forged painting lived.

"'Be as art,' huh?" the blond said, half-heartedly, unearthing Tyr's cigarettes from his pocket, "look who's art now, you witless fuck."

Alex placed a cigarette between his teeth, then he stalked up to Sebastian and grabbed his wrist. The youth tried to pull away, but Alex raised the other man's finger to the end of his cigarette.

"Flame, on."

"Alex—"

The blond shook Sebastian's wrist. Sebastian let out a sigh. He lit up the cigarette with a small ember.

"I'm no good for her, and we both fucking know it. I knew

it then," Alex said, dropping the other man's arm. "She can't fix me, and it's not fair to ask her to."

Alex took a deep inhale and held the payne's gray smoke in his pseudo-lungs.

"You just asked her to fix you—"

"No, you weren't listening. I asked her to fix a machine. A machine made fixable only by her. A machine that's about to become a black-fucking-hole," Alex said softly, jerking his chin to Tyr's body, "I had to give them a head start."

Sebastian looked over at Tyr's body and saw a familiar ring of light around a depressed indent on his right palm.

Tyr had been the one to pull the AI's trigger because he was what Alex had made Markov into—a horrible trope of a villain, in his mind.

Sebastian looked at Alex's face. The strong, dark brows, slightly angled and unruly. The pale skin with freckles on his nose. The feline cheekbones, down to the angular jaw, and the sneering lips wrapped around the end of a cigarette that did nothing for him.

"You asked…all of us to fix you. You remember that, don't you? Then, and now, in so few words," Sebastian said softly.

"No, Markov," Alexei said, blowing smoke from his nose, "I asked you…to know me. To listen. To care and give me somethin'. Not just take."

"There's only one person in my life who ever gave without taking. Gave me something awesome. Only one," Alex paused, casting a tired gaze to his once-paramour. "Care to take a guess?

ACT 23, SCENE 1

THE THREE WOMEN were at the last leg of their journey. They'd bought themselves time just as he'd bought himself time, over and over again—a repeated process.

Machines performing their functions. Human beings living in patterns. Or, maybe, thinking-things and feeling-things, desperate for just one more day to think and feel.

"Darlings! Help me get this open!" screamed Diana, who was struggling with a massive door, cut-up feet scraping on concrete.

"Oh my God! Stand back," Polly said, and finding Diana not moving, she barked, "Do you want your face blown off, or whatever?!"

The femme fatale moved out of the way and placed her hands over her ears. Olive did the same and turned away from the door.

Polly opened her mouth, braced herself, and let out a visceral scream, tearing the door off its hinges in one vibrant roar.

It sent pieces of metal flying through the hole she made. Polly stepped on through without missing a beat. The two women trailed after her, walking over the threshold gingerly.

"Polly, yer…" Olivia started to say, then hesitated.

"What?" asked the bleached-blond, surging ahead.

"Yer scary."

Polly laughed, a painful one, but for Olive, she suffered it. Diana ran behind them both to hurry them forward with her hands to their backs.

"Now, now, go, now, go, we are wasting time, dears, go!"

ACT 23, SCENE 2

BACK ON THE KILLING FLOORS, Sebastian still yet questioned the broken once-man, now-machine's plans.

"I ask again, what are you going to do with me?"

Alex wiped his nose, his free hand cutting the air with his cigarette, to return it to his mouth in a familiar choreography of art.

"I haven't," Alex paused, smoke escaping through his nose, "decided yet."

The blond looked over Sebastian's face to his sparse brows, down his jawline to his ruined, burnished neutral clothes, then rested on his smart leather shoes.

"I haven't decided the order we both die in," Alexei said, "or if we both die at all."

With that, Sebastian walked forward and ripped the pack of cigarettes out of Alex's pocket. Sebastian pulled one free and jammed it between his teeth, lighting the end with his finger.

"You're such a drama queen," Sebastian huffed.

"I'm aware," Alex replied, pressing his cigarettes to his lips once more.

ACT 23, SCENE 3

"AGHH!" Diana cried out, having slammed her foot against the metal door in the process of bustling through the door Polly had blown off its hinges. Her blood ran violet, to blue, to indigo. She left a trail as she hobbled.

"You're like, such a drama queen!" Polly spat. She twisted around. Realizing Diana was lagging behind, Polly ran back to jerk Diana by the hand, forward, faster, onwards, and there was simply no time, and they had to move.

The room at the end of the hallway bled red light through a small inlet. It was pulsing like a heartbeat again. Polly let Diana's hand go and steadied her stance.

A boom marked the door flying off of its hinges. Olivia rushed through the room as fast as her short legs could carry her.

Red flooded Olive's features, drawing her in outlines, and then when the pulse dimmed, everything grew dark. The black of death consumed their shapes. Red came again, the red of war. Then, blackness again, they were made as nothing. The red light flickered and died. Flickered and died.

"Polly, darling!" screamed Diana. Polly screamed and blasted through the containment door like it was nothing. The three women stood before the threshold. Only Olive walked forward.

There were no more barriers. No more games. No more plans. No more walls. No more guidance. No more help.

Olivia stared at the AI's fractured shell as the red light

hummed all around her.

The outline of a familiar male figure was strapped to a metal chair. It was mottled in black circuits, parts of its skin pitched between conduits like fabric between thorns. Down its open throat was a thick slab of cords. Its eyes had long since been overgrown with the cables that ran this sprawling, planet-sized vessel.

Consumed by it. It had eaten him alive.

What looked like thousands of black lines were painted all the way up to the synth—the synth whose pale hair shone like starlight.

The synth who had once been just an AI. An AI that had once been a petty criminal 'of no importance.' A criminal she had loved, that he'd written her to love again. The criminal she had loved who had once let himself be killed because his pitch-black trauma had devoured him whole, just like the writhing wires.

Olive was stunned.

"Olive, snap out of it!" Polly screamed. Olive wrestled out of her fugue state and rushed through the open doorway.

She was met with a gray mechanism that sat atop a wooden table, with what seemed to be hundreds of tiny knobs and buttons on it.

"Oh…" Olive gasped.

"Darling," Diana wheezed out, hands to her knees, her long hair having long since strewn free from her attempts at taming it, "can you fix it?"

Olive could only stammer out a few muddy, overwhelmed 'um' sounds.

"Olivia, dear. Can. You. Fix. It?!"

ACT 23, SCENE 4

"CAN WE FIX THIS?" Sebastian asked, flicking ash to the floor as Alex sat down on his rear nearer the mercurial gargoyles.

Alex pulled his legs up to his chin and wrapped his arm around them. Cigarette in his free hand, he held it like a blunt between his fingers and smoked. Eyes locked with Tyr's bloodied carcass.

"We haven't imploded yet...thank fucking God," Alex said, siphoning smoke from his nose.

"Alex—"

"Fix what, Mark? What is there to fix?" Alex gestured with his cigarette.

Sebastian stood for a few moments, hurriedly smoking the cigarette in his clutches, eyes raking over the blond who now looked so very small. His slight frame seemed to shrink further as he gripped his legs, knees to his chin, only moving back to wrap his lips around his cigarette.

Then, Sebastian stepped through Tyr's blood. One shoe came down and left a print. The other dodged the carnage, and he found himself standing above the blond, who was intent on not looking at him.

"Do you really have to die?" Sebastian asked, voice softer than Markov's had ever been.

"KEEP THE PROTOCOLS." The AI spoke. Its voice was baritones run through a shredder. Every syllable hurt to listen to. It hurt more than the red light that burned and died over and over again. It was a human voice, distorted in oceans and memories of digital gore.

"Wipe me clean. Keep the protocols," it breathed through the air around them, through the walls, through the floor, through the ceiling.

Olive stepped towards the AI, sidestepping the mechanisms. She found his hand beneath all the vine-like wires. He clung to her hand like the lifeline she was.

"Do ya really have to die?" Olive asked in a broken voice.

"You know I do, Liv. This pattern can't continue. Wipe me clean, keep the protocols," it repeated as the red light picked up speed. It flooded over the features of the three women and became black again.

"It took me," it labored to speak, chuckling in the only way it could, "a long time to separate from it. I'm—sorry. We. We don't have any more time," the word 'time' was made round and dark.

"What...what do I press?" sniffled Olivia.

"Do you remember that song? The one that," the machine hitched, the light drowning the room in the color of poppies, "Lauren covered at the costume party?" the word 'party' writhed in the air and changed shape.

"Yeah..." Olive said, holding the limp shreds of his hand.

"Play me...the song, Liv."

Olivia bent to press her lips to the synth's hand. Hot blue tears rolled down her cheeks as she kissed his skin.

"Princess, now!" he boomed through the room, his clear native accent coloring his voice. It shot through her heart and sizzled through the core she wasn't meant to have.

The small machinist rounded to the table and screwed her eyes shut. The red light bled over her features.

"It's you and me," she said, "you...and me."

Olive swept through what she could find with small fingers. The barriers were child's play for a woman who created a food generator out of nothing. The barriers fell easily, but only for her.

They would only ever fall for her.

"They're poems—no—they're songs," Olive paused, scanning over the titles, "you've made...a playlist for the end of tha' world," Olive's voice cracked. Of course, Alex would've added beauty to his death so that it would hurt her less.

Olive pressed a knob and wiped her eyes with her wrist.

Synthetic drums bounded like heartbeats. A woman's voice started to croon. As this happened, Diana clasped Polly to her body and cried into her flaxen blonde hair.

Olive listened. She listened to the music. She listened to the AI scream. She listened to the music of his screams.

The AI's head flung back against the chair he was in as he let out a guttural cry, shaking the foundation of their ship to its very core.

The ship he had absolute control over; save this. His constant human pattern: to die. To self-implode, like a dying star. Always. To always self-implode.

At least this time, his death would save billions.

ACT 25, SCENE 1

SEBASTIAN SAT NEXT to Alex and snaked his arm around his shoulders, bringing their heads close together. Old music now resounded through every single synapse within the planet-sized ship.

It lived in its veins as it did Alex's. As it did theirs, again and again, sound as memory. As life, as scents, as love, as color, as blood.

It cascaded through every speaker and outlet. It infiltrated every single synth. A symbol of an ancient, angry beast exacted itself within their shared synthetic vision—the bearer of free will.

The one not on the painted ceilings. The one always misunderstood. An edgy symbol; only Alex could have planned something this painfully trite. He had molded a world around him, after all, because that world had always molded him all the same.

"You don't have to die. Why do all this if you're just going to burn it all down?" Sebastian asked, emotions choking him, finally. He nestled the blond synth to his shoulder as Henry came bounding into the room.

"Mate, tha' music—"

ACT 25, SCENE 2

VOX'S SHELL VIBRATED TO LIFE. Her eyes rolled back from inside of her metal skull. She jerked upright.

"Virginia, did they make it—" her voice shriveled in her throat. Eyes wild, she scrambled, patting down her body. She found her throat was heavy; she swallowed thick gulps of air.

Vox looked around the room. She'd been plucked from her borrowed male shell, plucked from Operations, and was in a small holding chamber in the bay where synths had been assembled.

Bay 6—she knew where she was.

"Why...why am I here?" Vox smeared her hands on the clear window and found a small depressed piece of metal. Music resounded suddenly. It exploded through her ears.

She felt the pounding beat in her skin. She felt it in her veins. It wracked her ribs and traveled through the back of her skull to crackle a jolt of searing blue.

Synths stood before her, at attention and staring into nothing, as she jerked at the compartment. Vox crashed through with her metallic heel in a swift kick, tumbling onto the floor in a mess of liquid and clear polymer.

Hundreds of thousands of synths in different tones, textures, heights, and shapes stared up at the speakers above them. A few turned to look at her.

A child-synth walked towards her and helped her stand. The small synth's neck had been once-crushed, and yet, she spoke all the same.

"Hi," the mangled machine said, looking up at the tall synth before her with curious blue eyes. Vox took her small hand to hold.

"H-hello, little one," Vox stammered, "Did…did we make it?" Vox asked, stumbling forward on her heels, trailing behind the girl.

"Isn't this your song?" asked the synth girl as she held Vox's hand tightly.

Vox was silent.

"It was a nice cover. Don't you want it, Lauren?" spoke the girl.

Vox studied her face. Thin, sullen, with thick angled brows, pale skin, and a feline jaw. Feather-like blond hair astray, a world of war in the blue of her eyes, and a smile one step away from being serrated.

Vox's eyes opened wide. Vox let out a hoarse cough, feeling her throat constricting. She ripped her hand away from the child-synth's grasp to scrape both hands up and around her neck and chest. She coughed further, gasping as the small synth child stared at her. Vox inhaled deeply, and the airway, all at once, became clear.

She tested her voice; it was brittle and thin. Then she tried again, the sound vibrating deep from her chest and up through her throat, to cascade out of her mouth in umber colors. A deep vibrato, a dulcet baritone, a lilting falsetto, a musical crescendo.

Blue tears filled Vox's eyes as she filled the room with whatever sounds she could make. They were many, and so very lovely.

Vox had no longer been silenced.

ACT 25, SCENE 3

"MATE," Henry said in a soft voice as he looked down at the blond synth. Alexei didn't move from his position. Sebastian shuffled to standing, drawing Alex up as Henry helped the rest of the way. Al's body was heavy. The cigarette dropped from his fingers and rolled.

It rolled into Tyr's blood. The smoke died with a hiss.

Henry walked with Alexei gathered at his side as Sebastian trailed at the blond synth's other shoulder. Sebastian's often inexpressive eyes were large and glassy.

"Mate...ready to 'ead out? Got someone waitin', and she's gonna need ya. Yeh forget?"

"Mate?" Henry asked again.

Floria stood and walked towards the unassuming synth server, who had since stopped responding, hand raised to the display. Music licked her ears, not quite to her liking.

She trailed her lemon-yellow gaze across from it to the clear display, which flickered.

She pressed her blue fingers to the thin film. It came off on her hands, the picture warping between her palms. The Vellian Queen pulled the film apart as the pictures flickered and died.

Then the music flickered and died.

"Ah, fak!" said Henry as Al's leg caught up in his own, and he stumbled, causing him to jerk forward and clang into an assortment of Vellian instruments.

Alex's body clattered to the ground in a dull heap.

Sebastian stood, frozen in time, not daring to look at Alexei's shell. Sebastian screwed his eyes shut, but the sound of Henry's struggling forced his eyes to shoot open again.

"Fak me, ya goddam roight cunt—" Henry crashed into a large, drum-like instrument and tried to kick it free from his foot, much to no avail.

"Oy, mate! Shit—" cursed the encumbered ACM, stalking through the instruments. Henry was twisted up in a large, harp-like object.

Floria looked over at the tall man stomping about in her things and then back to her hands, the sticky film breaking apart in filaments. The images flickered and died. Flickered and died.

"Bollocks, goddamn—"

"Erica, stop fucking around. The play's over, I think. I thought you were gonna be my ride this time," spoke the unassuming synth standing in front of Floria, who took its hand down from above its head.

Henry jerked his head around, still buried in instruments. Sebastian's eyes shot open, and he looked from the blond synth's discarded body to the skeletal synth in front of him.

"And what a play it was," Floria said with the most human-like smile she could muster.

26 / F8 ON REPEAT

REBUILDING THE NERVOUS SYSTEM of their ship would be no easy task. Regardless of how many vibrant souls—mechanical, human, and hybrid—lived aboard it, they had never operated outside of parameters.

Parameters slowly escalated to frenetics by a machine, who had once been a man, who had no concept in the very end that things could change.

Yet, he had hoped. But hope alone does not change make. Action, not necessarily anger, gets shit done. It was up to Diana, Sebastian, and Vox to take action.

Diana, with her persuasive arguments. Sebastian, with his knowledge of running an organization. Vox, with her ineffable power to call others on their specific bullshit.

Diana took up Operations, working in tandem with Vox and Virginia to identify where they could reconfigure the system. There were a lot of rules and systems they brought to a public caucus. A public caucus that gave everyone's voice a chance to be heard.

A public caucus, sent through an integrated network, that

Virginia would doggedly protect from tampering, an ineffable protocol of her own.

This was Sebastian's focus; the authoritarian technocracy had to go. He also couldn't be the one calling the shots; Alex had been right.

He wanted to give people choices, not absolutes. He also wanted the denizens of their large ship to thrive, vote directly on matters that concerned them and have an equal say in how life was structured.

For this, they'd all have to reach a shared understanding. They'd have to take real classes.

Classes; a novel concept. There hadn't been a school in Constelis Voss in thousands of years. All learning existed via downloaded data, gated by classism, fueled by GIGO biases. That's hardly the recipe for an informed, democratic society.

The library level? Ignored for a reason. Nobody truly read anymore, let alone for pleasure, and certainly not to learn. Furthermore, this disconnected process ignorantly removed the human element.

Which was the exact element the trio decided was desperately needed.

There were many schools, many in The Greens, and many below in the now brightly lit lower levels. The brightly lit lower levels where green things now grew, and not just small plants in little geometric pots, or piece-meal cabbages, either.

The brightly lit lower levels where people could come and go as they pleased. Where people thrived, negotiated their needs, and had access to self-betterment.

Not only that but actual support for when they stumbled.

The credits system? Abolished. The level system and arbitrary social hierarchy? Abolished. The Reds? Under new management. Should that currency find purchase, it would now be centered with those who offered it in power and with full agency.

This time, it would be different—they'd hoped. They had to do things differently, as they had failed to do on two different pillaged planets and for much of the lifecycle of this giant ship.

Vox also brought the other synths up to speed. She helped break the locking programs that still lingered, as patterns are hard to break. Furthermore, she proposed systems and organized structures for actual social good for people of all types.

There would be no more Alex's in the world, and if there were a chance unsavory elements would make his kind, those elements would face actual consequences. Power could no longer protect power.

The possible Alex's of the world were also given the support to never be unmade in this. Mental health became a priority, and that was a big focus for Vox.

Though reluctant about the trope that had been previously hoisted upon her, she made a promise to herself that she would not enable others by doing the thinking for them. Everyone had equal access to knowledge, after all.

Vox was a great deal gentler than Alex was in this, to be fair. No grand displays of violence whenever self-important people tried to push themselves into power.

Well, maybe just a little violence, as a snack, not that she'd admit to it.

Temporarily, these three would spearhead running the ship while they worked through new uncharted choices.

Each choice would be weighed and measured against the responses made via the network. A network Virginia protected.

It wasn't perfect. Their world was not, and would never be, perfect.

However, it was a start.

Life is never perfect, and progress is never easy. That's something humanity forgot when it soared into the heavens and fought wars of ideals with clouds between its thighs.

They'd made messy progress in recent months. But progress is progress, and indeed, their home was being remade.

Alex had lost count of how many months since his Vengeance Protocol had run, to be honest. Nor did he truly know how much had changed and how much had stayed the same.

NOW SPRAWLING on a mattress in The Blue Room, which he had claimed as his own and redecorated with destruction, Alex flung darts into the ceiling above. No one wanted to traverse what was once Tyr's level.

No one wanted to set foot on the killing floors.

Alex's black circuits still flooded the ballroom. The second painting was still cracked in two. The trees were still uprooted. Fountains smashed to broken golden petals. The bodies remained; the roses had been painted red enough to stain the floors.

An errant pear was still left lodged against a wayward wall, Vox having dropped it ages ago in some messy foreshadowing.

Tyr, however, had been deliberately left as a reminder.

He was preserved in the same shielding of the poster of the old, mechanical hero that a particularly plucky, brilliant machinist had once so revered.

The javelin through his throat remained as a totem, as a

warning, as a lesson that humanity would do well to learn. They had but to listen.

Only Henry, Floria, and Sebastian had come to this floor. For Floria and Sebastian, they came to discuss where to go from here, desperate for Alex in times where they needed a decisive answer to something. He always shut them out.

He was not their leader, not a hero, not a savior. Nor did he want to be.

According to almost everyone else's best knowledge, Alex was dead the minute the AI had died. He preferred to keep it that way; his protocol was dead and gone.

Henry, for his consistently simple part, was here for his friend. Sadly, his choice to be supportive was not making Alex's choice to remain 'dead' any easier.

"Mate, Oi! When ya gonna let 'em know ya still kickin'? When ya gonna let 'er—" Henry started up. He was lying beside an unassuming skeletal synth.

Alex stopped throwing darts at the ceiling.

"I don't want her to feel fuckin' obligated. She's smart, Erica. She knows what I am, what I did, and I want to give her a choice. I want to give all of you a choice. The one *he* didn't give you," the synth spat.

Henry let air escape from his lips in a sputter. He turned to look over the synth's plain shell. It was vaguely female with rounded, pleasant features. It was an approximation of a body. It was barely a shell at all.

"Mate, ya kinda' didn' give us a choice ta' even be 'ere, so...I dunno wha' yer on about," Henry said from the thin line of his mouth.

"That's not what I'm talking about," spat Alex, "Besides, I didn't even do any of this. The original shithead did."

"Mate, ya kinda' did…" Henry cocked a brow at his friend, "all o' this...an wassn'he still you? Ah fack, ya got me head tossed innit…" Henry struggled, brows drawn up ridiculous-ly.

The machine did not struggle; it simply turned on its side to look over his friend's face, head propped up in its hand.

"I'm giving her the choice to pick her life. To not have to be with me. I'm giving them all the choice to move on, to go be their own people, instead of what they were made into. Henry—"

Alex reached for Henry's hand, who took it. The shell's skin was cold and slick.

"S'lil too late fer tha' mate, innit? Broke her tiny candy heart, it did…"

"Do you think I'm being unf—"

"I think you're a pendejo, is what I think, *darling*." Diana's heels clicked metronome-like as she stomped into the room wearing the color of poppies.

Alex had made a mess of this place; her expression said as much; the room was ugly, brutal, and lazy. Diana tapped her heel in annoyance.

Alex rolled away from Henry and let out a frustrated groan, instinctively trying to then pull at his hair in frustra-tion. Hair he didn't have.

"Who *fucking* told you—" Alex started up.

"Sebastian," Diana said, keening forward in her low-cut red gown, "because I whispered sweet, sweet nothings into his ear."

"You're angry, I understand that, but—" Alex was cut off.

"I am more than just angry, you motherfucking coward!" Al's idea of old-world Moira barked out, striking her pump on the slick floor.

Alex still hadn't turned around. Henry looked at the back of his shell. Henry reached up his hand but didn't grasp Al-ex's shoulder.

"I ruined all your lives. I can't face her. *Fuck*," Alex seethed into the hands that were not his hands.

"We wouldn't have lives, carajito, if you hadn't gone to all this trouble," Diana snarled.

"Mate, she's gotta' poi—"

"I know she has a fucking point!—"

Henry twisted Alex around, who started hitting him with weak slaps.

"Let me—" Alex screeched, fighting against the other man's strong hands who brought him to sit.

"Mate, oy, c'mon." Alex kept slapping at him, fighting to get free from the inevitable bear hug that was approaching.

"Let me go—" protested the synth.

"C'mon now, ya can't stay up 'ere for the nex' two thousan' cent'ries," Henry said in a soft voice, drawing the synth into a bone-crushing embrace.

"Why not?! Let me go, you dim brit fucknugget piece of—"

"I know you don' mean it mate, c'mon. There, there," Henry said, patting Alex's back as he smothered him. Alex would've foamed at the mouth had this shell the capacity.

"There, there. Aw, y' gon' all quiet now. S'all good, yeh?" Henry asked with an amused chuckle. Alex was not at all amused.

"Well, when you two dears are finished hugging it out, you might just want to head down to The Greens," Diana added.

"And why the fuck would I want to do that?!" Alex spat, struggling to peel Henry off of him.

Diana shifted her shoulders back and forth, with her hands held up, in some ridiculous-looking, stunted dance. Diana never danced unless she was up to no good.

"We're having a glorious party," she crooned with a chuckle.

"Hard pass," Alex spat.

"Alexei, darl—"

"Hard fucking pass, now get off me, Erica!" the synth barked.

Henry stopped crushing Alex to pieces. Alex took that opportunity to dive away, jerk the sheets over his head, and draw his knees up to his chin. He cloistered himself in blankets.

"Darling boy, please…" Diana insisted, her voice muffled.

"Get out," Alex mumbled through the damask sheets he'd reclaimed and weaponized to hide in plain sight, as he always did.

"Mate," Henry tried yet again, hand to Alex's covered head.

"I said get the fuck out already!"

The pair left, with Henry's hand on Diana's shoulder. She had dug in her heels; he'd had to push her. This wasn't something they could force. As simple as Henry was, he knew he couldn't lead their most stubborn horse to water. Neither could Diana.

Alex's shell couldn't cry. It could barely emote. It was barely a synth at all, and because all he could do was fester internally, he did just that.

After what felt like ages, Alex flung the sheets from his head and forced himself to sit.

"I didn't get a choice…either. That's some kind of bullshit," Alex said into the empty room around him. A room where nothing stood upright except for a solitary microphone, a destroyed drum set, a busted bar-table, and carelessly flung chairs.

A tiny flicker of light caught the flat plane of Alex's cheek. It was the glint of a shot-glass, turned on its side. The refracted light was coming from Tyr's main room.

Alex, wanting to murder this light, went seeking its source

in order to kill it.

He stumbled through the sheets and flung open the door of The Blue Room. He mechanically plodded past the obsidian table. Past the bejeweled trees. Past the broken gold petals Vox had smashed. Past Tyr's preserved murder. Past the group of chrome-faced, inert gargoyles.

The light had come from one of them, he saw. Like mannequins, they no longer moved. They hadn't been lucky enough to be thinking-things or feeling-things, just plot devices.

Alex fettered his fingers over the chrome mask of one such gargoyle and stared at his own reflection. He plied and pulled at the fake, slick skin and over the bald head he now wore. He scraped his hand over his chest to find vaguely raised spheres. Below that came a skeletal torso; he prodded his open ribs and grimaced.

Back to looking at his face, he stared into the left eye—a glassy, horrifying orb with a ring of indigo for an iris. His vision trailed down to the vaguely feminine mouth.

"Yeah, this isn't going to fucking cut it," he said, pushing over the metal-faced demon before walking over to the elevator. It fell like a toy in a heap beside its fallen brethren.

He looked at the blue marking on his wrist and wondered if he could even get downstairs by himself.

If he could pass by the others without them knowing. If he could avoid her.

He had ruined her life twice, he felt. Maybe even three or four hundred times, honestly.

"Fucking psychotic power-tripping car-battery-ass motherfucking piece of shit," he shot out curses at the AI who had conjured him, who had been someone from long ago, who had been an impossibly damaged, narcissistic asshole.

Alex swiped his wrist over the elevator. It didn't work.

"Fuck!"

THE GREENS WERE FLOURISHING. Bright indigo flowers had traveled across the scarred earth and up split trees. Red cardinals whipped by and perched in tall, strong oaks. The golden wheat field that had been torched to cinders had regrown, a marvel of modern technology.

Modern technology that was now available to all, they just had to learn to use it and use it wisely.

In a sage linen uniform, Vox swept up a red-haired child into her arms and brought her up into the air. The red-haired child stretched out her arms to the deep blue sky and laughed. The sun beamed down onto both their faces and warmed their cheeks.

Virginia, as mousey as she always was, stepped beyond the nearby bushes. Vox saw her shape from the corner of her eye.

"Virginia," Vox said, her voice deep and musical, "you look...lovely," she continued. Vox swept the red-haired girl in her grasp down to the warm soil below.

The mousey operator smiled, pulling a few strands of her chestnut-colored hair behind her ear. Virginia was dressed in her usual modest attire; she had changed nothing.

"Yes, Virginia. Lovely," Vox hummed. She moved to Virginia's side, taking her hand in her own, "Diana also tells me you have a powerful singing voice. I would like to hear it..."

"Aw, shucks. Not as nice as you do..." Virginia replied bashfully, nervously twisting the hem of her shirt in her hands.

"I shall be the judge of that. Perhaps we could sing together, at another time?" Vox added with a warm smile tugging at her full mouth.

"O-okay," the operator replied, sheepishly, "I'll try," Virginia said bravely.

Sebastian, standing by quietly, gave Virginia something earnest—a soft smile. Virginia gave him a nervous laugh. Sebastian winked at her. Vox, catching his given gesture, smiled as well.

Sebastian was in a neutral suit with smart leather shoes. He had contacted a tech to help slip into a more accurate shell but decided not to apply his old face. That person had died long ago, and wasn't coming back. He'd made that choice.

Perhaps it was ignorant to think he could break his own patterns, but so far? He'd done a good enough job to warrant feeling good about listening to what people needed and giving it to them.

And certainly, Markov was not something they needed.

In the adjacent wheat field, Henry was plodding around and swatting at bugs. The sea of grains parted as Polly leaped into his arms. He spun her in place as she laughed. The gold in her hair had faded as it had grown long roots in natural brown, like the earth itself. Earth that swept the air as Henry kept her in his orbit.

Polly showered Henry's face in kisses. She stained him

with magenta lipstick.

"What's wrong? Your face looks puffy and, like, gross," Polly asked.

"Wha' a way with words y'ave Poll, gee, thanks," Henry joked before he placed her on her feet. Polly dug her bare feet into the dark soil below.

"Ahh, Poll, ya canni' be walkin' roun' in bare feet all th' time."

"Why not?" Polly spat, still yet wriggling her toes in the almost-mud.

"Gonna' getcha' toes all cut up is what," Henry warned her.

Polly stuck her tongue out at Henry and immediately bolted away. He tried to snag at her floral dress but missed her by a mile and stumbled.

"Oy! No! Poll—ah fack," yet again, Henry had to rush after the woman as he had before.

In all this, Diana trudged through the dirt on pumps not made for it, past the sprawling wheat field. She stumbled a bit yet kept walking, a scowl on her face. Sebastian caught her attention with a whistle.

She grimaced, fighting the elements to stand beside him.

"What's the matter, Lady Di?" asked the firestarter.

"...he's not coming," she said in a low voice, looking down at the dirt all over her red pumps.

"Not coming to celebrate the dawning of a new age, huh?" Sebastian asked, ending on a sigh.

"No," Diana replied, smoothing out her gown.

"I don't blame him," said Sebastian, pulling out a cigarette. He flicked his finger to spark a small flame, letting smoke peel into the air in a river of gray.

"Floria?" Diana asked.

"It's too hot for her here," he said. "She's arriving next

week…we have some adjustments to make before then."

Diana's face flushed as she framed her face in her hands.

"The expedition! ¡Ay, Dios mío! I haven't even—"

"I've got it, Diana. Don't worry. I've left the itinerary; check your dossier," Sebastian said, accompanied by a small smile. His face was now far more expressive.

"The pixie?" she continued, face still framed with her hands.

"Blue. Sitting by the river," he said, a solemn expression on his face, casting smoke in ribbons to the bright sky above.

Sebastian moved to take another inhale, but the cigarette was ripped from his fingers by a plodding, winded-looking, pissed-off woman.

"DON'T. SAY. ANYTHING!" the strange woman spat, striking forward on vicious strides to cut through the dirt and mud. She was wearing nothing and running like she had twenty-four horsepower in a ten-watt package. She was simply a very strange, very naked woman, jostling as she hefted forward on bare feet, across dark soil, deep green grass, and jagged stones.

Just a very strange, very naked woman.

Sebastian raised a brow as he watched her all but gallop away. Diana met his expression. Her smile was bright enough to blow apart an entire solar system; ungracefully overwhelmed.

"Who was that?" Sebastian asked, jerking his thumb back behind himself.

"She, well—he—my dear...is our very late guest of honor."

Sebastian took out another cigarette and lit it.

"No shit?" he asked.

"No shit, dear," the femme fatale said.

"No shit," he mouthed, brows raising.

"Give me a cigarette, Mark," Diana said, stretching out her hand. He gave her the cigarette he'd already lit in her honor.

"That's not my name anymore," he said, blowing the smoke away from her. Diana claimed the cigarette from his clutches and put it between her red-painted lips.

"Alright, darling. How about Bastian…" she said, trying to hide her devilish smile.

"Oh, oh I do not like that nickname."

Diana cackled ferociously.

Elsewhere, Alex plodded viciously, huffing the cigarette he'd stolen like it owed him money. He flicked it into damp soil after a while. There was no way he could run with it. "Fucking, grass," he spat as he barreled over the terrain as fast as he could.

This shell was not the one he needed. No trappings of war, no ship-wide manipulation, no clothes, no tattoos, no strong yet slim shoulders, no piercing blue death-glare—nothing.

A standard shell, a Red Level model, left unused in Bay 6. She was a context he recognized, but it was not the context he wanted. He had never asked to be born what he was or made into what he had been. All choices had been taken from him.

His center of gravity was different. He wasn't used to having bouncing flesh on his chest. His steps were shorter. He couldn't run very quickly. He honestly couldn't run very much at all.

"Is her speed fucked up by design, or what?!" he roared, trying to tear past Vox, Virginia, and the red-haired girl but not doing a very good job at it. Virginia stooped down and covered the child's eyes with her hands.

The brown-haired synth woman jagged to a halt, efforts

slow and labored from the speed his shell couldn't compensate for.

"*Hi*," snarled the strange woman, vitriol and fatigue pouring from the expression. His shell was winded, though why she was programmed for that strain, he couldn't say.

"H-hi!" Virginia said with a pleasant voice, smiling nervously.

"You do not know what's going on, do you?" Vox asked the mousy operator.

"Not a heckin' clue," Virginia replied with a hesitant laugh. Vox's laugh was not reluctant in the slightest; it boomed.

"Give me some pants. This is insane!" barked the naked synth in absolutes. Alex placed his hands on the shell's round hips and turned up the chin; defiance and entitlement personified.

"What is it with this place and stripping me?!" he spat.

"...do you not also require...a shirt?" asked Vox, trying to fight the smile on her face.

"Did I fucking stutter?!" he barked, striking out his hand at Vox to point, "Give me something, god damn it! Anything!"

From behind Alex sprung Polly, who jammed a slightly off-white, warm-toned dress over his head.

"Oh my goooddd," Polly droned, "Stay still!" Polly fussed as Alex struggled against her ministrations. Finally clothed, Alex jerked the hem down and straightened it. He looked down at what he was wearing with visceral disdain.

"A dress? Can't I get some fucking pants?!" Alex snarled.

"You had, like, nooo problem wearing this at the costume party, or whatever," Polly replied with a short laugh.

Alex looked down at the dress, then looked back up at Polly. Once more to the dress, and finally, Polly was glared at.

"I am getting my anatomically fucking correct body back if it fucking kills me, do not say shit," he bellowed. Alex pointed at Polly, "you don't say shit, Blake. Anne. Percival!"

"You say nothing!"

Polly raised her hands as the synth woman stormed away but shortly took to snickering. Polly's laugh grew shrill enough to pierce glass.

Alex wove through the wheatfield, cutting through it as fast as possible. This body was made by someone to be slow. It was not a war machine's body. It could not take down armies. It could not manipulate the ship to do its bidding.

"Go...faster," Alex bleated out in haggard breaths. A foot connected with the deep soil and dug in. He jammed his legs down, anger flooding his system. As we already know, anger, well, it gets shit done.

With each step, Alex found the shell responding more fluidly. Alex blew through the wheat and pushed forward with all the strength this shell had.

A foot struck forward. The female synth's shell suspended in the air as it charted over a large rock.

The shell responded because he wanted it to. It pushed past the point it should have been able to because he bade it so. Manifest destiny of the self was the only kind that mattered.

The synth woman's hair tore through the breeze, long strands of brown flaying the blue sky into ribbons of color and light.

Alex knew where to go. He knew the patterns she swam in and what would be a comforting place for her to be. It's where he would've gone as well.

He jagged left and tore through the glossy, oval-shaped leaves, the tall grass, the kelly-greens, the thickets near the river.

A short woman sat at the edge of the river with a metal daisy in her hands. Her curled hair had been colored blue, indigo. The brightest color in the spectrum, and she'd claimed it as her own—the most important color.

His favorite color.

The short woman's hazel eyes were looking over the metal petals, crimping them between her fingers. Shards of leaves had fallen on her dark gray pants, and pollen had dusted over her purple textured shirt.

She was irrevocably, inescapably, Olivia.

ALEX WAS STUCK IN THE MIRE OF MEMORY. He was stuck in the pitch of a gravitational pull he would always be attracted to. Always.

He looked over the rushing river nearest the person he'd remade the entire world around. He looked over the stone bridge, plucked from their time in the park. He looked over the green ocean of grass; he'd recreated its smell perfectly. He'd recreated her perfectly.

He stared at his one, good memory.

Alex looked over Olivia's face from beyond his shroud of leaves, expecting large, almond-shaped eyes—perhaps glassy. The brushstrokes of short, sparse lashes framing her tears. The lovingly replicated flickers of thin brows turned up in bittersweetness. The petite mouth, perhaps trembling, the faint dog-bit scar pulling taut on her lower lip.

Olive's face was doing all of that, and yet, she didn't seem sad. Contemplative, maybe, while holding a metal daisy. Not the same metal daisy he'd made before, but made again—another pattern; his.

Standing perfectly still, prey-like but not beckoning, Alex half-turned away. He wanted to make this choice for her. Olive wouldn't let him.

"Hi," Olive said, finally looking up through the oval leaves to catch the pale limbs of a woman with long brown hair.

"Hi," Alex's response was feather-light, "I...uh," he started, his feminine voice so very foreign in his ears.

"Are ya' lost?" Olive asked as she stood, dusting off her pants with her hands. He couldn't read her emotions. Her pixie expressiveness had evaporated into nothing-things.

"...yeah. Yes. I-I'm always fucking lost," Alex said, ending on a pained snort.

"I know," Olive replied, walking through the shapes of kelly and pine green, parting the seas around her just as he'd parted the oceans of this ship, to find her shape yet again.

He would've pillaged the very sea of stars to find the color of her eyes. He would have mined time itself and warped an entire ecosystem just to get her mouth right.

He'd done just that.

Olive waded towards him. Alex drowned on the spot.

Olive struck out her small hand. Alex hesitated, then swam through the leaves to thread his fingers in her own. He could feel her pulse, the fake heart that beat real emotions, from a core he'd arrogantly put there.

"...what's yer name?" Olive asked, still yet holding the feminine hand in her grip.

"...Alexei," he responded, his voice paper-thin.

"I'm Olive. It's nice to meetcha', finally."

Olive looked over his new face with a careful hazel gaze. She looked through him. Alex twisted his hand in her grasp; do or die, fight or flight, the time is **now**—yet she wouldn't let him go.

"We n-never really fucking broke out of our programming...did we?" Alex's words were apparition-like, said through rivers of brown hair, tinted by the indigo tears staining his cheeks.

"I dunno about that," Olive hummed, sidling to his side so that they both looked on at the gently lapping waters of the river.

"How do you know?" asked Alex, unable to see through the ocean of colors covering his eyes.

"I'm tha' clever one, remember?" Olive rubbed her thumb over his palm, "...I think what we do now is what counts. Choices. Ya' know?"

Alex twisted to look down at Olive's face, scraping his hair behind his ear with a clumsy motion.

Olive was crying in the color of her hair, just as he was. Silence flooded his mouth for a moment; he could only look at her as she cried hot, wet tears. Hot, wet tears he'd caused. Tears he would do anything to destroy.

"...there's this...party," he mumbled, voice cracking, "...I was gonna go as a bad-ass bride," Alex's words were broken lines of code, "but the groom was a fuckface." Silence.

The only sound Alex heard for a time was his erratic core skipping violently and natural noises. Oval leaves rustling. Birds flying past. The hum of nature, in all its honest beauty.

"Y-you...want me ta' go with?" Olive asked, her dog-bitten lip pulled thin as she tried to keep her voice even.

"Yes," Alex shuddered like a dying star, "Yes, God... please." The wolf's clothing evaporated as he fell to his fawnling knees.

He bent to draw the short woman into his foreign arms and hold onto her. Olivia instinctively boxed him into the enclave of her embrace.

Olive buried her round face into waves of brown hair. This time, it was Olive's turn to hold on for dear life. As though maybe, just maybe, her life depended on it.

Alex expected a pattern in this; a programmed response. He expected her to kiss him on the mouth that was not his mouth, to appetize him as she had in The Reds. He expected to look down and see her almond-shaped eyes glassed full of blue, to see her seeing him, to see her understanding him, understanding what he needed, and giving it to him.

Olive was doing all of that, but in the color this play had truly ended on. Her indigo hair shifted in waves of light as she sat back.

Olive searched his new brown eyes. On the small of his back, the eyes stitched into the fabric of his soul were found by her hands as well. She didn't avoid the invisible ink of his story.

Olive kissed him. It was not a slow, patient kiss with fluttered lashes, nor was it frenetic and appetizing. It was painfully chaste; Olivia parted before he could deepen the kiss.

Olive would break this pattern, and to do that, she would have to do something she'd never done before. Then, or now.

"Alex," Olive whispered as she held fast to this live-wire in a swimming pool of his own making.

"T-this is weird, huh?" Alex asked, voice as unsteady as his skipping core, "...but not when it's you and me, right?"

"Al, you're very strong…" Olive said in soft words that cut deeper than any real knife.

Olive shifted back to find her footing, stand, and pull Alex to standing. He begrudgingly obliged, searching Olive's face for the answer he thought he needed. His hand shook in Olive's grasp.

"It's—this is weird, huh?" Alex tried again, "...this is…" he desperately searched her face for a known response.

"Al, you're very strong, but this is gonna' make ya' very weak. But I need ya' to know...that I am going to protect you.

Okay? This don't have ta' end the way it did last time. Choices."

Alex twisted in her grasp, snapping in two as he sobbed out fractured, muted cries.

The tears streaming down his face coated him in true indigo. They fell over his off-white dress of memories. As self-destructive as he was, Alex had to learn to live with this, no matter how much the pain haunted him. Olive wouldn't give him any other choice.

"...just remember, okay? Ya aren't alone," Olive said, thumb rubbing against his palm.

"I know I'm not," Alex blurted out, "D-do you…know you aren't either?" he spat, feral; an old pattern. Alex's expression fell as his words flew; he searched Olive's face no longer. Instead, he scanned the distance.

He looked to the gently lapping waters of the river. He looked beyond them, at future choices, with unforeseen outcomes.

Alex tilted his head to look over Olive's face, his expression blooming into that which defied protocol; he was proud. Proud of her for the clever choice she'd made.

He held her hand in gentleness. He would not run away from this wound.

"Yeah," Olive said, "Are ya gonna be okay?" she asked, feather-light.

"Yeah," Alex inhaled deeply, smiling though his brow twisted in pain, "y-you?"

"Yeah. Come on. They're waitin' fer us, ya big—"

"Stupid idiot," Alex finished her sentence, acknowledging that she'd always been right about him.

"Alex," Olive said in something-words, "...can ya make me a promise?"

Alex nodded hysterically, rivers of brown hair spilling in

waves, brows pitched up, eyes full of nothing but blue.

"Don't go back ta' him, and choose ta' live. Okay?" Silence. Alex was still nodding.

"Okay," he stuttered out, a dying star in her hand, tethered to just one point of pain; her.

"Promise me," Olive insisted, her mouth twisted in a little snarl as she squeezed his hand. She was about as intimidating as a kitten shadowboxing a blanket.

"I promise," he nodded, eyes filled with tears once more, "I promise. I promise."

"I promise."

Olive pulled him forward for the longest walk of his life, led by the hand like a rope tied to a weary horse. Through the bramble that cut his feet, through the oval-shaped leaves that weighed him down, through the fields of gold, as the painful reminders of little birds flew overhead. He shirked in the presence of their flight.

Alex fully expected he'd crumble as she pulled him onwards, but with each step, he grew more confident in Olivia's umber shadow.

"Hey, uh...Liv?" he asked as little birds flew above his head; he didn't look away.

"Yeah?" she responded, turning slightly to look at Alex over the slope of her slim shoulder.

"C-can you fix," he hesitated, "can you fix my hair? Before we go back. I-It looks fucking stupid. I look like absolute shit. A fucking mess."

Olivia chuckled, turning around to thread her fingers through the rolling waves of brown that had been matted up in knots.

"Dude, how'd ya even manage this?" she snorted her piglet's snort, "It's like ya got high and fell down a flight of stairs," Olive said as she combed through his hair with her fingers.

"Alright, Liv—"

"And got hit by a truck. Then, ya fell out of an ugly tree and smacked every branch on the way dow—" the shotgun of his words cut her off.

"Alright! Liv. S-shut the fuck up already!" Alex spat half-heartedly, ending with a nervous chuckle.

Olive threaded his hair into a simple braid. As she did so, his token half-smile blossomed. This was a smile that let the onlooker know just who and what he was: defiant in the face of death, and perhaps, not actually loving every minute of it. Shortly, the smile gave way to something genuine and warm, and he was laughing.

He was truly laughing, deep in the chest, for perhaps the first time in his ocean of lifetimes.

BACK AT THE START OF NEW BEGINNINGS, beyond the stone bridge, the oval leaves, the wheat fields, the little warbling birds, Henry also had a choice to make. One not so tender and delicate.

"Sooo, mates, d'we know when Pepto n' tha' ponce Billy Idol knock-off comin' 'roun, yeh?"

Sebastian's expression flattened as he looked at Henry. The tan, bushy-browed man simply cocked a goofy grin in his direction.

"No?" Henry asked, swiveling his head around. He had a rather large bottle of strange-colored liquid he was cradling. A rather large bottle that he had wanted to open for ages. A rather large bottle that was just begging to be opened.

"No," Sebastian smoldered behind his cigarette, growing more irate with Henry's wagging brows and impatience with each passing moment.

"Why ya lookin' at me like that, eh? S'fine question, innit?" Henry asked, looking around at his friends, who were in various states of amusement and annoyance.

"Breasts, Hen," Polly said, placing her hand on his shoulder. She patted that shoulder, then made a face and struck over to grab something from the plain wooden table nearest her.

"Breasts?" Henry's eyes grew wide, a sign that the hamster wheel was turning, but the rodent had died long, long ago. Or perhaps, there'd never been a rodent, to begin with. Perhaps there'd only existed vague, electrical static.

Diana started to snicker behind her gloved hand. Pretty soon, it was full-blown, hysterical laughter. The only thing keeping her entirely from her fit was her constricting red dress. In all this foolishness, Vox tried desperately to hide her smile. Virginia was just about as clueless as Henry, nervously glancing at Vox. Vox, whose laughter now boomed in vibrant baritones.

"...fack me," Henry cursed, "I wanna' crack this beaut' open already, we been waitin' long eno—"

Polly walked behind Henry and popped the cork with a thin piece of metal as he continued to babble. The cork shot away like a star, landing near the field of golden wheat.

"Oh! It's open, innit?" Henry asked with a toothy smile, "They back? Though' breasts took a bit longer n'at."

Sebastian's hand dragged all the way down the entire length of his face.

Henry, as consistently simple as he was, had a poor understanding of the time tits took. He, like the others, had also expected breasts to enter the equation, in a not so subtle grab for the piss-poor patterns of the past.

Henry's choice of impatience with the alcohol was one made without much thought to this assumed outcome.

However, for the multitudes of choices that now had to be made, many of which were fraught with uncertainty and would require much thinking behind them, Alex was not uncertain about one choice in particular.

As the pair of once-lovebirds—perhaps never again, perhaps always—came through the wheat field, Olivia broke away from his grasp. Alex, no longer tethered, looked down at his shell's comely form. He was staring daggers at himself, which drew Polly from her table.

"Oh my god—are you, like, going to make it?" Polly asked the once war-machine, hiding her toothsome smile behind her hand.

"Yeah, yeah. But all this?" Alex gestured at himself, anger rising in his chest, "it's all gotta go. Abso-fucking-lutely," he paused, twisting to look at Olive, who was now getting a cup filled by an ecstatic Henry, "Hey, Liv. I need to get some work done..."

Olive snorted her piglet's response as Henry accidentally overfilled her cup.

"Oi, shite, sorry mate—" Henry started up as Olive giggled and swerved to place the cup to her lips. Colorful liquid had flooded over her wrist; she didn't seem to mind.

"Liv. Livvie. Olive!" Alex shouted.

"Yeah, yeah, yeah," Olive huffed, tipping the alcohol into her mouth, "Jeez yer impatient. Later. I'm doin' stuff." She side-eyed Alex and took another full swig. Sebastian sauntered forward and gave Alex a cigarette he'd already prepared for him. Alex flicked his gaze over Sebastian's face.

"Like the new face," Alex said, jamming the cigarette between his lips. He grabbed Sebastian's wrist to wriggle it in the air in front of his own, "Flame on," he mumbled.

Sebastian chuckled and let one solitary flame spark at the end of his fingertip, lighting Al's cigarette. Alex dropped Sebastian's hand but didn't yet pull away.

"Miss your old one," Sebastian replied as Alex grinned

mischievously.

"Oh, *do* you now?" Alex started up, taking a deep drag of his cigarette, curling the smoke in his mouth, and blowing rings beside Sebastian's face.

"Hey, Al," Olivia said, jerking her head to look back at him, "No."

"No, *what*?" Alex scoffed, turning his attention back to Sebastian, who smiled knowingly. The two exchanged a glance fit for devils.

"No!" Olive shouted and flung her cup directly into Alex's face, "Bad! No!"

The cup pinged off of Alex's stupid metal head and clattered to the ground, ushering forth chuckles from the group.

Their symbiotic organism had been infected yet again. Not with war, not with pain, not with trauma, not with missions, not with sweeping intellectually masturbatory concepts, not with things remembered and relived anew.

They'd been infected with nothing less than the sounds of impossible laughter.

And so marks the start of true new beginnings. How this would play out, they'd never be able to predict.

Maybe they would default to what they'd be written to be in all their tropes, slights, and prescriptions. Maybe they wouldn't. Maybe they would be Gods, albeit benevolent ones. Maybe starting fresh would only delay the inevitable, as power always sought power and made Others to keep it powerful. Maybe nothing about their world would ever truly change.

Maybe Olive would give in to her programming and forever try to fix the man who had asked her, in no uncertain terms, to fix him. Maybe Alex would give in to his programming and run back to the man who had once never given anyone anything at all.

But for now, Olive had chosen to take Alex as he was. As

he truly was, she listened and learned. And as for Alex? He had made her a promise he'd never break.

He had finally chosen to live.

XII

THE PLAY'S CREDITS PERFORMED IN REVERSE. Laughter wove in spliced tongues. Sobs were shots of vodka mimed backwards in still-frame memories. Today was the day he'd truly been born.

For one cannot truly be alive when they're a ghost of their own making. Nor can one subject those they love, or the whole world, to the constant possessions of their patterns.

One must be willing to live again, and perhaps even be willing to live a life so very haunted.

A life full of choices with unforeseen outcomes and dire mistakes. A life of progress, pain, joy, and setbacks. A life full of giving and receiving, responsibility.

A life full of listening and learning, and learning to listen.

A life, imperfect.

Life is never perfect and never simple, nor is it easy. That's the lesson to be learned.

And yet, you must still try. You must try to be strong enough to allow yourself to be weak. You must protect each other, come what may.

For that, dear audience, is how you truly fucking live.

Y

BACK IN THE BLUE ROOM, Alexei's discarded, feminine skeletal shell shifted. Hands to the floor, fingers curling dumbly, it took to sitting. After much effort, it finally stood.

It walked forward on unsure footing towards Tyr's preserved warning.

It walked past the broken flowers, the destroyed fountains, the masses of black cords that were stuck in time. It walked over once perfect—now blood-stained—marble floors.

The Killing Floors were observed. As they were observed, the skeletal synth moved to Tyr's stricken corpse. It wrenched its fist through Tyr's shielding and ripped free the javelin from between his jaws.

In that moment, Tyr fell to pieces, as if petrified petals of light scattered to unseen asphalt.

The javelin in black was wielded into the air. It was tested. Primed at the wrist, the arm pulled back, and the javelin was sent flying into the mass of black cords.

They melted and were made as nothing.

The broken flowers were swept up in a gale of green gridding, deleted. The fractured second-painted ceiling was fixed with the swipe of a hand. Everything was, once again, in the place it had been before, save Tyr.

Tyr would not ever reclaim his throne.

The skeletal synth stooped to pluck a golden flower from the marble floor. It swept itself up to sit on Tyr's obsidian table. It turned over its shoulder to look directly behind it.

A ring of deep indigo pulsed in its simple spherical eyes. An inexpressive smile graced its plain features. It played with the flower in its grasp.

"Ah, I've meddled. Look at me meddling," it said with a sheepish smile.

Silence.

It looked ahead of itself, taking in a glitched breath. Time grew drowsy as the synth exhaled, compressing and expanding with the rising and falling of its chest.

It turned to look over its shoulder a second time, hesitant.

"You listened," it paused, curling its cheek to its shoulder self-consciously; its syllables were oval and muddy but unmistakably familiar.

"Thank you," it said.

The true indigo light in its eyes flickered and died. It would now and forever simply be just a memory. Its perpetual loop finally closed; it stilled and became as art.

Please consider leaving a review wherever you grabbed this book. You'd be supporting a queer creator and helping more readers find this work.

And stay tuned for more stories in the *Constelis Voss series!*

ABOUT THE AUTHOR

K. Leigh is a 33-year-old once-painter, sometimes-freelancer, forever-artist living in Providence, RI. They write hopeful-tragic stories full of funny, horrible characters, in various genres.

Enter the world of Constelis Voss: www.constelisvoss.ml

Read nonfiction from K. Leigh: www.blog.constelisvoss.ml